Kitsune Enchantment

by

Margaret L. Carter

Kitsune Enchantment

Cover Art by *Jennifer Greeff*

The Wild Rose Press, Inc.
PO Box 708
Adams Basin, NY 14410-0708
Visit us at www.thewildrosepress.com

Publishing History
First Black Rose Edition, 2020
Trade Paperback ISBN 978-1-5092-3317-5
Digital ISBN 978-1-5092-3318-2

Published in the United States of America

Dedication

With thanks to the members of online critique group
TWWS
for their continued advice and support

He cupped her cheek with his free hand. He leaned in, giving her plenty of time to draw back if she chose.

She didn't. Instead, she parted her lips, waiting. His lips brushed hers. The heat spread over her whole body and flared at her core. His tongue teased hers, and she twined one arm around his neck. Her nipples peaked and tingled. Twisting sideways to close the space between them, she couldn't suppress a sigh of pleasure when he drew her into a loose embrace that tightened as she snuggled up to him.

Her eyes drifting shut, she ran her fingers through the dense pelt of his hair while he deepened the kiss. Waves of sensation rippled through her. As she moved her hand downward to skim over his cheek, fuzz tickled her palm. Whiskers? Surely she would have noticed if he'd been unshaven. Besides, this growth felt more like velvet than sandpaper. She opened her eyes.

Ryo flinched and pulled back. In the twilit dimness relieved only by the light from the overhead fixture just inside the door, his skin definitely looked lightly furred. Not only that, his teeth looked, well—*sharp*. She scooted to the end of the couch.

Ryo snapped his mouth shut and covered it with one hand. Springing to his feet, he mumbled, "Sorry—not feeling well all of a sudden. I'll see you tomorrow morning. Sorry!" He scurried to the bathroom and slammed the door.

Staring after him, Shannon stood up, suddenly lightheaded, and gripped the back of the couch to steady herself. *What's gotten into him? And his ears—why do they look the wrong shape?*

Chapter One

As usual, holding human shape for an entire day in the near-constant presence of other people had strained Ryo's control. He didn't bother changing out of the slacks and polo shirt he'd worn to work but hurried out back as soon as he got home. Alone in the tiny yard behind a six-foot, wooden privacy fence, he unlatched the gate so he'd be able to push it open without hands to go for his evening run. At last he allowed himself to relax. His ears lengthened and perked up, pointed and furry. His teeth sharpened into fangs, while a plumed tail sprouted from his backside. He crouched on the ground. A familiar voice shattered his focus.

"Ryo? You back here?" Footsteps paced around the outside of the house. "I rang the bell, but I guess you didn't hear it. I came by to drop off your courier bag. You must've accidentally left it in the office. I don't live that far out of the way, and I figured you might need it between now and the next time you come in."

Damn. Joel Brady. Can't let him see me. Joel occupied the cubicle next to Ryo's at the company they worked for, Delmarva Game Galaxy. Since Ryo mostly telecommuted and wasn't scheduled to be on site again for almost a week, he couldn't deny bringing him the bag was a nice gesture. Still, damned inconvenient timing. Shapeshifting in this sheltered spot had always been safe enough that he'd obviously become complacent. He forced his mouth to form intelligible words. "Thanks. You can leave it on the front porch."

"What the heck, I'm here now. Let me just give it to you."

The latch clicked, and the gate started to open. "No need." Ryo's voice came out as more of a growl than human language. He struggled to wrench his half-transformed body back into man shape.

"You okay, Ryo? You sound sick." The gate swung ajar. About the same age and height as Ryo, but huskier, the unwanted visitor had a mop of sandy hair trimmed to just above his collar and wore wire-rimmed glasses. Ryo froze and stared up at him.

The blue eyes behind the glasses widened in shock.

The change swept over Ryo like a gust of wind. His clothes vanished to wherever they went on such occasions. He shrank from man-size to twenty pounds as his face became a muzzle, his hands and feet morphed into paws, and a reddish pelt covered his skin. Stunned, both he and the intruder gaped at each other for a second.

Joel broke the silence. "Good God, this is actually happening. You really turned into a fox."

Ryo sprinted for the open gate, tripping Joel in the process. The other man dropped the black courier bag and yelled after him, "Hey, wait, I won't hurt you!"

In blind panic, Ryo rushed around the house with Joel lurching after him. From the corner of his eye, he glimpsed Joel getting into a car and starting it. Ryo ran up the street, pursued by the vehicle—a two-door compact of some light color—his animal vision couldn't distinguish exactly what.

After running two blocks through the quiet

neighborhood of sixty-year-old houses similar to his own, he gathered his wits enough to think of leaving the street and cutting through yards instead. *Can't go home now. Need a safe place. Where?*

He zigzagged under trees and through hedges, abruptly shifted course whenever he hit a fence, put on a burst of speed when a dog barked as he ran past its yard, and skidded to a halt at an intersection with a four-lane road blocked by speeding vehicles. Glancing behind him, he didn't see Joel's car. Fragmentary scraps of human thought reminded Ryo to wait until the light changed to let him cross without getting flattened. He imagined drivers and passengers exclaiming to each other, "Wow, look, a fox in broad daylight," and snapping photos with their phones.

Where to now? Inhaling the auto fumes, he abruptly sensed something else, not exactly a smell, yet something beckoned him, wafting on the air. Like magnetism, it drew him across the road onto a tree-canopied, two-lane street that led into a community more upscale than his own, though apparently not much newer. Grateful for the fading of the gasoline and smoke stench, he followed the lure of the strange-yet-familiar energy. Suddenly he knew what he was sensing. *Magic!* He quickened his pace again, to first a trot, then a run. *Got to get to it. I'll be safe there.* He sprinted along the sidewalks, now heedless of the risk that some curious resident would catch a glimpse of him.

Panting, his legs aching, paws sore from the pavement, at last he reached the spot the magical allure emanated from. He found himself on a short, narrow side lane lined with the same kinds of ranch-style and split-level houses as the rest of the neighborhood. Mature trees shaded the yards, and freshly mown grass tickled his nose. One of those houses looked familiar…

I've been here before.

He'd eaten a meal there as a guest not long ago, in his human body. The magical aura didn't glimmer around that dwelling, though. The energy drew him to the house next door.

As he approached it, a tirade of furious barking burst out on the other side of a chain-link fence one house farther down. A dachshund flung itself against the barrier, proclaiming its indignation at the wild beast intruding on its territory.

Ryo's heart raced with fresh alarm. His human mind knew the dog couldn't get through the fence and probably wouldn't be a match for a fox anyway, but his animal self wouldn't listen. *Danger! Dog!*

He dashed to the front steps of the magic-haloed house and stopped to catch his breath. Next door, a woman's voice called, and the dog wheeled around to run toward her. Ryo shuddered in relief.

A small figure materialized on the porch in front of him—a slender, white cat wearing a red scarf around her neck. With a grave nod, she greeted him in Japanese. "Welcome, *kitsune*."

Her melodious voice soothed his panic. With as much of a bow as he could produce in fox shape, he answered in the same language, "Profound thanks, *bakeneko*." Even if she hadn't spoken, he would have instantly recognized her as a cat spirit, just as she'd realized his nature at first glance. Therefore, she understood his speech, which would have sounded like yips and whines to an ordinary mortal.

"Come up and rest." She flicked her tail and sat down next to the front door. "What brings you here in such haste?"

With another word of gratitude, he climbed the three stairs and stretched out on his belly a few feet from her. "A man was chasing me in a car, but I'm pretty sure I've lost him." Now that his animal flight instinct had faded, he reconsidered Joel's unexpected visit. The two of them didn't know each other well enough that Joel would impulsively drive out of his way to return an object that would have been safe enough in the office. And considering the route Joel would have normally taken, Ryo did live out of the way, even if not much. *Does he suspect there's something abnormal about me?* "Until just a minute ago, I didn't know where I was going. I followed the magic I sensed and ended up here." His lips spread in a vulpine version of a smile. "Now it's obvious why."

"It is not only because of me. This house holds a scroll that was once enchanted. Although its power has drained away, some residue lingers." She inclined her head to him again. "My name is Yuki."

Ryo introduced himself. "You live here?"

"The master and mistress kindly share their home with me." A tinge of humor crept into her voice. "As does their cat." At the rumble of a car engine, she glanced toward the street. "Ah, here they are."

A sports car pulled into the driveway behind the hatchback already parked there. Two people got out, a tall, lean man with seal-brown hair, who wore a naval officer's summer white uniform, and a strawberry-blonde woman. Ryo suppressed the urge to flee again. Now that the panic-induced fog was fading from his brain, he recognized Thad and Val Garrett. He recalled they were almost newlyweds, just married in January. On Memorial Day, he'd met them during a cookout at Thad's parents' house next door. He'd gone as a guest of Thad's cousin Shannon McBain, Ryo's partner on a crowdfunded graphic novel series.

Halfway up the sidewalk, Val stopped short. "What's that? A dog?"

Thad, too, halted in mid-stride. "I don't think so."

She clutched his arm. Even from a couple of yards away, Ryo's vulpine ears picked up the acceleration of her breath and heartbeat. "Um, there's a fox on our porch."

"Roger that, it's a fox, all right. A big one. Yuki's with it, though, so it must be harmless."

Ryo couldn't blame them for their nervousness on finding a twenty-pound fox at their door. He sensed their gradual relaxation as they scanned him, doubtless taking a closer look at his dark copper fur, white-tipped, plumed tail, and black paws, muzzle, and ear tips. It struck him as odd that the endorsement of a bakeneko—spirit cat—made them more comfortable with him.

Yuki greeted the couple as they walked up the porch steps. "Good afternoon, Valerie-san, Thad-san."

Val stared at the fox, her breathing not quite calm yet. "Who's this?"

"He fled here for refuge because he sensed traces of magic. I trust you do not mind."

"No problem, if you vouch for him," she said.

"He is not an ordinary fox. He is a kitsune."

Val translated the exchange for Thad. Ryo wondered why she understood the dialogue while her husband didn't.

"Kitsune—fox shapeshifter," Thad said. "Come on in, no point standing around out here."

"More magic?" Val muttered as she unlocked the door and walked into the foyer. "I thought we'd finished with that." As Thad held the door ajar for Ryo to enter, she blushed and said, "Sorry, no offense meant."

Ryo answered with a yip he hoped sounded friendly.

After depositing his hat, car keys, and briefcase on a small table just inside the door, Thad led the way to the living room. An ordinary cat—a long-haired, silver-gray tabby—lay sprawled across the cushions of an armchair. He bristled at the sight of fox-Ryo, hissed, and ran away. Val and Thad sat on the couch with Yuki between them, her tail curled neatly around her front paws. He said to Ryo, "Can you change to human form? That would make it easier to talk."

In full agreement with that point, Ryo hesitated anyway, since he hardly knew these people. He cast an uncertain glance at Yuki, who said, "Have no fear. They can be trusted."

He willed himself to shift. His two hosts' stunned expressions blurred before his eyes as he made the transition. Having sometimes watched himself in the mirror, he knew they saw his outline waver, expand, dissolve, and re-form, with a pale glow shimmering around him. He knew his eyes kept their amber hue in both shapes, while his triangular, sharp-chinned face hinted at his fox nature. His slightly wavy, short, dark hair had deep red highlights that also reflected the coloration of his animal form. Not that anyone who didn't know the truth about him would guess those connections.

"Ryo Larsen." Thad waved to the armchair opposite the couch. "Good to see you again, though I wasn't expecting it to be in a situation like this. Have a seat."

Taking the offered chair, Ryo allowed himself to relax as he recalled their first meeting. He'd been reluctant to accept Shannon's invitation to the Memorial Day family party. Crowds unnerved him and stressed his ability to control his shapeshifting. To his relief, though, he hadn't needed to face a crowd, only Thad's parents, Thad, Val, and Shannon. The hosts didn't have a dog or cat to react with alarm and hostility to Ryo's hidden animal side. He'd lounged in a lawn chair under a fragrant magnolia tree, enjoying conversation and bloody-rare hamburgers with no unpleasant surprises. Not once had his human shape threatened to disintegrate.

The others had relished the spicy tofu and sweet red-bean rolls he'd brought as his contribution to the meal. Sure, the lore about kitsune having a special fondness for those foods was a cliché, but it was also true. Thad, his folks, and Val asked intelligent questions about Ryo and Shannon's graphic novel series and didn't seem bored by his answers, even when he got carried away and ran on at elaborate length about the complications of translating character and story ideas into e-book form. He left the party wistfully imagining he might someday get closer to Shannon than their current, mostly online, collaborative friendship.

His thoughts snapped back to the present when Val asked, "Can I get you anything? Water or tea or something?"

The question reminded him how parched his throat felt from the frantic run. "Water would be great."

When she returned from the kitchen with a tall glass of ice water, Thad said, "Sorry, but as an engineer I have to ask. How do you have clothes on when you turn human? Where do they go when you're a fox? Not to mention all the extra mass? According to the basic laws of physics, the first time you ever transformed should've set off a nuclear explosion."

Ryo shrugged. "Magic. As far as I can figure out, that stuff disappears into a pocket dimension until I change back." He gratefully accepted the glass from Val and took a long drink. "Thanks. I raced here all the way from my house in Eastport."

"As a fox?" She resumed her seat on the couch. "Why? If you don't mind talking about it?"

"Simple. Joel, a guy I work with, accidentally saw me changing, and I panicked. As Yuki mentioned, I instinctively headed for the magic in your house. I must have subconsciously sensed it when I was next door with Shannon on Memorial Day." He sipped at the water and set the glass on a coaster on the coffee table. "With luck, maybe he'll decide he imagined the whole thing."

Val asked, "So you're like Yuki?"

The white cat herself answered, "Not precisely. I am a cat with the power to become human. Ryo-san is a man who sometimes becomes a fox."

Val translated the reply for Thad. "Makes sense," he said, "from what I know about kitsune."

Ryo recalled hearing about Thad's tour of duty on a ship stationed in Japan, which accounted for his

9

knowledge of the folklore. "Technically, I'm only half kitsune. My dad's a retired American naval officer, and I was born in this country and grew up with ordinary people, so most of the time I think more like a human than a fox." Ryo hesitated before asking a question of his own. "I can't help wondering why you're not more shocked about me and how you ended up living with a cat *yokai*." That word, which had no single English translation, referred to a wide variety of spirits, demons, and other supernatural beings.

"Complicated story," Val said. "Yuki woke up from an enchantment when I accidentally broke the spell on a Japanese scroll I inherited from my grandfather. Next thing I knew, the house became infested by magic and besieged by a wolf demon." She smiled at Ryo's blank stare. "I told you it was complicated."

"That's why Val can understand Yuki's speech and I can't," Thad put in, "because she's the person who activated the scroll."

"So we're surprised to meet a fox shapeshifter," she said, "but not totally mind-blown. Does Shannon know about you?"

Ryo gave an emphatic shake of his head. "No way. Aside from my parents, nobody knows except you two." He sighed. "And now Joel, maybe. I hope he'll decide he was hallucinating."

Val frowned thoughtfully. "You aren't planning to tell Shannon? Not that I know her all that well yet, but she doesn't strike me as the kind of person who'd react well to a guy keeping a dark secret."

"She'd think I was either putting her on or flat-out crazy. If I proved it with a demonstration, she'd probably freak. Either way, I'd lose her. Lose her friendship, I mean." As much as he wanted more, he feared risking even that by pushing for a closer relationship.

Yuki's mouth quirked in a feline approximation of a smile. "He has a point, Val-san. Not everyone shares your openness to the supernatural."

Ryo finished his glass of water and stood up. "I better get going. By now Joel must have given up and left when he couldn't catch me. Thanks for the hospitality."

Thad said, "Let me give you a lift. No point in walking a couple of miles back home in this heat."

"Great, I won't turn down that offer." After farewells to Val and Yuki, Ryo followed Thad out to the car. Their acceptance of Ryo's double nature, an unfamiliar experience for him, warmed him to the core. If only he had any hope of the same response from Shannon, he might consider sharing the truth with her.

****

At 6 p.m. on Friday, Shannon McBain turned the sign on the door of the bookstore to "Closed" and joined the owner, her friend Elena Salazar, in the combination office and break room in the back of Twice-Told Tales. *I wonder what this is about?* They didn't usually hold meetings at the end of the work week. Elena, a tall, slender woman in her thirties with her black hair worn in a single long braid, waited in the chair behind the desk. The grave expression in her brown eyes wasn't reassuring.

"Have a seat. We've got to talk." She gestured to the shabby armchair nearest the desk.

"That doesn't sound good." Shannon moved a pile

of paperbacks from the chair to the floor and sat down but didn't relax into the sagging cushions.

"I'm afraid not." Elena sighed. "You must have noticed what's been happening to our profit margin."

Shannon nodded. She could hardly help noticing. In the eleven years since she'd started working at the bookstore, first in summers during college, then as a full-time employee, and now as assistant manager, she'd seen internet businesses cutting into their sales. The store had started as a used book shop before expanding with new titles as well. Without the ability to pass along deep discounts, no quantity of book launch parties and local author signings made them competitive with online convenience. *I guess this means no raise this year.*

She braced herself for that news but gaped in dismay at Elena's next sentence. "There's no viable choice but to close the shop."

Shannon drew a long breath and let it out in a whoosh. "Are you sure? When?"

With a wry smile, Elena said, "Not today or even next week. I'll plan on six months from now, when the lease comes up for renewal—with a probable rent increase."

Only six months to find another job. Shannon's head reeled. "Have you told the others?" Two young men who worked part time between classes, just as Shannon originally had, were their only other staff members.

Elena shook her head. "I'll talk to them Monday."

"I can hardly imagine this place not being here." Shannon looked around at the fridge, microwave, and lunch table in one corner, and at the comfortably overstuffed shelves on the opposite wall.

"Neither can I. I fully expected to run it for the next twenty or thirty years, then turn it over to the next owner—maybe you, if you were still around."

They'd casually discussed that possibility several times before. A pang of regret pierced Shannon at realizing that future would never come to pass. "What will you do?"

"Sell off as much inventory as possible." Elena waved at the open door to the adjacent stock room. "Then move the business online. That way, I won't need to pay for retail space or staff, but I'll still probably have to get some kind of day job. I'll miss you."

"And I'll miss you."

"Of course, it's not like we'll never see each other. We'll keep getting together for lunch or whatever."

Shannon nodded. Still, she knew their friendship wouldn't stay the same once the work connection ended.

After a subdued goodbye, she picked up her purse and walked out. On the way to the exit, she couldn't resist pausing to inhale the reassuring scent of new books and scan the familiar rows of shelves, with a glance at the archway leading to the used-book section of the store. *Only six more months of this.* The humid summer heat enveloped her when she stepped outside. Still struggling to absorb the shock of the announcement, she headed for her compact car in the parking lot of the strip mall. Not a glamorous location, but a fairly affordable one with the bonus of some impulse traffic from the other stores in the complex.

Not my worry anymore. I'd better start considering where I go from here.

Chapter Two

As Shannon drove homeward down Route 2 with the air conditioner on the highest setting, her thoughts revolved like a hamster on a wheel. She hadn't applied or interviewed for a job since her sophomore year of college. The prospect of entering the job market, effectively for the first time, at the age of twenty-nine made her pulse race with anxiety. She'd known Elena as a family friend for years before the offer of a part-time position, since their fathers had worked together. Shannon had loved the bookstore work from the beginning, and after deciding against graduate school, she'd segued smoothly into becoming a full-time employee. *What else am I supposed to do with a degree in English lit? I guess I've got six months to figure that out. The clock is ticking.*

She swung into a fast-food drive-through a block from home and minutes later pulled into the parking spot outside her one-story apartment in Severna Park, the end unit in a row of six. A crape myrtle tree, festooned with pink blossoms beginning to shed their petals on the sidewalk, shaded the front door and offered an illusion of shelter from the heat. She hurried into her much cooler apartment. After changing into shorts and a T-shirt, she carried her chicken sandwich and diet cola into the spare bedroom furnished as an office. As soon as she opened the internet browser, she yielded to her worries and ran a quick financial check. The figures in her savings account and IRA looked no more reassuring than the balances on her credit cards. Because of the damage her father's gambling addiction had done to the family in her teens, fiscal security topped her priority list.

I do have one more income source to fall back on, at least.

Not that she could dream of living on the crowdfunded graphic novels she coauthored with Ryo Larsen. However, a recent development gave them a chance to make a significant profit from those works. Six Continents Media had expressed interest in mass-producing their books and had hinted at offering a contract. If that prospect came through, Shannon's half of the advance could provide a comfortable cushion for job-hunting. The deal depended on the meeting she and Ryo had scheduled with Harvey Wright, an editor from Six Continents, next weekend at ContrariCon, a science fiction and fantasy convention held just north of Baltimore. For the dozenth time, she silently prayed to make a good impression on him.

She opened the unfinished file of the latest adventures of her character, Golden Raptor, and Ryo's, Crimson Vixen. Just as Raptor took the form of either a man or a giant eagle, Vixen alternated shapes between woman and bipedal, human-size fox. Shannon wrote the action and dialogue based on plots the two of them brainstormed together, and Ryo, who had a day job with a game design company, created the art. Now she paused on an image of Raptor in mid-transformation from man to bird of prey. As usual, Ryo portrayed the shift in an ethereal style that made her feel the magic could actually happen. The discreet but sensual glimpses of Raptor's nudity in human form didn't hurt. Opening a separate window, she typed the next few pages of dialogue that she'd been mulling over through the afternoon, before Elena's bad news had overridden thoughts of fantastic quests.

Within a few minutes, the signal for a new instant message dinged. *I should've remembered to turn off the sound. Shame on me—distraction bad, concentration good.* She couldn't resist checking, though, and was glad she had when the transmission turned out to come from Ryo.

"About the con this weekend," it started.

Oh, no, he isn't sick or something like that, is he? I can't meet, greet, and negotiate all on my own.

"I don't really have to be there for the whole con, do I?" the message continued. "What if I just drop in on Saturday long enough to meet the editor with you?"

She crumpled a napkin in her left fist, heat flooding her cheeks. *Don't even think about letting me down!* She typed simply, "Why can't you be there the whole weekend?"

"I'm not much for socializing, and I've got a project for work I should be catching up on. I trust you to speak for both of us."

"Not good enough," she tapped out with furious speed. "We can't predict how often or how long Wright will expect to talk with us. How do you think he'd react if you bail? Anyway, you're not leaving me to cover our dealers' room table alone without a better reason than that." *This is all I need, right after I hear I'm about to lose my job.* She considered adding that complaint to her message but decided she didn't want to sound as whiny

17

as she felt.

"You feel that strongly about having me there the whole time?"

"You think?!?!" She let her anger boil over in an eruption of punctuation.

After a long pause, he answered, "Okay, if it means that much to you, I'm in. I'll show up as scheduled on Friday and stay the weekend. Word of honor."

"I'll hold you to that." Did that mean she was important to him as more than a collaborator? Despite all their virtual conversations over many months, she still couldn't be sure.

After that heated exchange, she lost all motivation for composing a heroic scenario. She typed a few more sentences, then closed the word processor. She sighed over Ryo's illustrations for a minute longer before closing that file, too. *What's with him constantly trying to get out of social obligations? Is meeting people that awkward for him?* She could understand if he suffered from agoraphobia, but she'd seen no evidence of such a condition, and surely he could trust her enough to say so instead of inventing excuses.

They'd met at a convention in Washington two and a half years earlier, and he hadn't shown any signs of distress about being there. The video game company he worked for as a graphic artist had assigned him to a shift staffing a sale table. At the adjacent table in the dealers' room, Shannon had been helping a friend sell fanzines, some of which included her own stories about Golden Raptor. Ryo had bought one to read during lulls in customer traffic. To her surprised satisfaction, he mentioned that he'd already read some of her fiction online and become fascinated with Raptor, an eagle shapeshifter who'd accidentally crossed over to Earth from an alternate world after a magical cataclysm.

Casual conversation had led to a late dinner after the dealers' room closed, followed by hours of brainstorming about future adventures. At first Shannon had wondered about ulterior motives on Ryo's part, but he hadn't tried to hit on her at any point during the conversation. He proved himself genuinely excited by the story they'd concocted on the spot, giving Raptor a companion Ryo insisted the character needed. Thus they'd generated Crimson Vixen, a female fox shapeshifter who'd fallen through the same dimensional rift. Although the two characters hadn't known each other in their original world, they'd become first reluctant allies and then friends. The next logical step, according to Ryo, had been a website dedicated to a graphic novel series about the pair. By the time they'd parted at the end of the con, not only had Shannon committed to the plan for *Raptor and Vixen*, she wouldn't have minded a more-than-friendly gesture from Ryo after all. No more than a couple of years older than Shannon's late twenties, he stood only a few inches taller than her own five feet six, just the proper height for the hugs and kisses she caught herself fantasizing about all too often. She also imagined stroking his wavy, short-cropped, sable hair, so like a wild animal's pelt. Most alluring was the unusual color of his eyes, a golden brown that looked amber in certain lights.

Since that weekend over two years earlier, Shannon and Ryo had shared hundreds of e-mails, multiple cloud-based documents, and countless late nights of live chat elaborating their imaginary world. They also spent hours discussing everything but their personal lives—books, movies, TV shows, role-playing games, and the latest internet memes. To her delight, their opinions about such things, as well as politics, meshed well enough to allow lively arguments without hostility.

Yet their face-to-face meetings could be counted on two hands with fingers left over. She couldn't help wondering why, considering they lived less than half an hour apart, he in the Eastport section of Annapolis, she in Severna Park on the other side of the Severn River. Soon after their first meeting, they'd arranged to get together at a comic convention in downtown Baltimore. They'd driven separately and bought one-day tickets for Saturday. Come to think of it, at that event she'd gotten the impression Ryo didn't feel comfortable in crowds. He acted more relaxed when they retreated to the video room, where they spent most of the day binge-watching complete seasons of anime series and munching on popcorn. At the end of the day, they picked up sandwiches to go from the convention center snack bar and ate on a bench outside, dissecting the films they'd seen. Later, though, when she'd offered a tentative invitation to get together closer to home, he'd turned her down. Why did he seem to enjoy video chats and online work sessions with her, yet evade real-world interaction?

Although she suspected he found her as attractive as she did him, he didn't make any romantic overtures. She'd been pleasantly surprised when he actually accepted her invitation to the Memorial Day cookout at the home of her aunt and uncle. Ryo even contributed food to the potluck meal. As far as she could tell, he had fun, with no symptoms of social anxiety. She'd sampled his spicy tofu with some trepidation, relieved to find it had a pleasant zing but not scorching heat. Val, Thad, and his parents—Shannon's aunt and uncle—liked it, too, judging from the empty tray left at the end of the meal. Ryo instantly connected with Thad over their shared enthusiasm for anime and manga. Shannon basked in the shade next to Ryo, listening to him explain their graphic novel projects to the others more clearly than she'd ever been able to. At least, his presentation riveted their attention in a way she couldn't manage, and the questions they asked reassured her they weren't just being polite. When she drove him home, he said he'd had a great time in a tone that sounded genuine.

When she dropped him off at his place, he leaned toward her, his hands lightly resting on her shoulders, as if about to kiss her. At the last second, though, he drew back. After that, any hope she might have cherished for a breakthrough to a new level in their relationship seemed to have fizzled. A couple of weeks later, she'd invited him to spend an evening at her place outlining the latest book, and again he'd politely declined, on the grounds that he might be coming down with a cold. Since then, he'd continued to insist collaborating over the internet worked fine for him, with the excuse of not wanting to put her to extra trouble.

Doesn't he have feelings for me, after all? Or is he hiding something that has nothing to do with us? Maybe an old breakup that's left him cautious, like me? Enduring her parents' marital strife because of her dad's gambling, even though they'd eventually reconciled, had made her hypersensitive to evasion and possible deception. From her glimpse of Ryo's house when she'd picked him up for the cookout—a single car in the driveway, no hint of a second occupant during her few minutes inside—she was sure he lived alone. Even if he had a significant other, why wouldn't he mention that fact? He'd have no reason to conceal a relationship from her, since they were just friends.

No matter how much I wish we were more. Oh, stop obsessing like a teenager with a crush.

****

All weekend and into the next week, Ryo brooded over the upcoming convention. He couldn't blame Shannon for insisting that he pull his weight at ContrariCon, but the prospect loomed over him like a thundercloud of impending disaster. Representing his company for a few hours now and then, as he'd done at the con where they'd originally met, was one thing. He could put up with a short period of sitting at a display table surrounded by people he would likely never see again. But almost three days in the near-constant presence of a woman who turned him on? There Shannon would be, right next to him, with a snug T-shirt showing off her softly rounded curves, a miniskirt or tight jeans drawing his gaze to her legs, the sharp scrutiny of her hazel eyes focused on him, her auburn hair either tied in a jaunty ponytail or rippling to her shoulders... *Stop that!* He didn't have a snowball's chance of maintaining a continuous grip on his shapechanging power with that kind of distraction. At times like those, his alleged gift, as his mother labeled it, felt more like a curse. Maybe he could think up an excuse to duck out of most of the con without offending Shannon. *Right, who am I kidding?*

When he managed to stop worrying about ContrariCon, his thoughts reverted to the problem of Joel Brady. On the following Wednesday, Ryo's next day at the office instead of working from home, he tried to stay out of Joel's path. He succeeded until he left his desk late in the afternoon and headed for the elevator, only to find the corridor blocked by the very man he wanted to avoid.

"Ryo, just who I need to talk to."

Ryo couldn't quite make himself shove past Joel. "What for? I'd like to hit the road before the traffic gets bad."

"Come on, I'm sure you can guess what I want to discuss—what happened last week at your place. I know what you are."

Ryo's pulse accelerated. "I have no idea what you're talking about."

"Sure you do." The other man smiled as if inviting him to share a joke. "I saw you change into a fox."

"Are you kidding or just losing your mind?"

With a glance down the hall, where two women were rounding the corner toward the elevators, Joel said, "You don't want to talk about this where anybody could hear, do you? Let's go someplace private." He clutched Ryo's arm and steered him toward the nearest vacant conference room.

Ryo let himself be steered, not eager to have his coworker raving on about magical transformations in range of potential witnesses. *What can he do to me right here, anyway? Maybe I can convince him he imagined the whole thing...*

Leaning against the window frame, he warily watched Joel, who took the seat at the head of the table as if preparing to chair a meeting. "Give it up, Ryo. I wasn't high on anything. I know what I saw."

"Sounds like your reality check bounced. You saw

me, and then you saw a fox. I don't know what made you imagine some kind of connection." He kept his hands relaxed at his side rather than clenched and drew slow breaths to calm himself inwardly as well as outwardly. *The last thing I need is to sprout ears or a tail with him staring straight at me.*

"We spend most of our waking hours on video games about wizards and monsters. Why shouldn't I have an open mind about the supernatural?"

"You really believe this?" Ryo tried to echo the other man's casual tone.

"I'd rather believe you changed into a fox than think I actually have gone crazy." Joel leaned back in the chair, his gaze fixed on Ryo as if expecting the change to repeat at that very moment. "I've been reading up on kitsune. Fascinating stuff, including little details like their favorite foods being tofu and red bean paste. According to the folklore websites, you've got some amazing powers."

"So work them into a game. Which you seem to be confusing with reality."

Unfortunately, the repeated denial didn't deflate Joel's confident manner. "The legends mention a lot of other abilities besides changing shape. Foxfire, invisibility, possession, and a bunch more."

"If I could turn invisible, the first thing I would've done was dodge you."

As for fox possession, when Ryo had discussed it with his mother, she had warned him as a teenager not to try. "Until you gain much more experience, that would be dangerous for you. It is too easy to lose yourself in the mind of the person you attempt to possess, unless you have a companion to support you—ideally another kitsune."

"But you're the only kitsune I know," he'd said.

"A human partner would do, if you find one you can trust completely." Her wistful tone gave him the impression she'd never found one, even in marriage.

He had little hope of forming a bond with any such person, and it certainly wouldn't be Joel. Ryo started toward the door, but Joel stood up to block him.

"Don't be that way. I don't mean you any harm. There's something I'm hoping you can help me with, if you have those powers."

"Stipulating for the sake of argument that you're right about what you claim you saw, it doesn't matter, because I wouldn't be able to do most of those things. I'd be only half kitsune." He edged around Joel, who didn't stop him from reaching the door this time. "What do you want anyhow? Planning to sell this wild tale to a tabloid or monetize it on the internet somehow?" He stalked out of the room and headed for the elevators at a brisk walk.

Joel followed Ryo onto the elevator, vacant except for the two of them. "Hell, no. What kind of friend would that be?"

So now we're friends? Funny way to show it. "Again, what do you want?" Ryo jabbed the button for the parking garage.

As the elevator descended, Joel said, "In my research, I ran across the concept of *kitsune-mochi*."

Oh, hell. So that's what he's after. Clinging with an increasing sense of futility to his play-dumb strategy, Ryo said, "You expect me to automatically know what that means?" He did, of course, from the lore his mother had taught him, but he hoped to throw Joel off balance.

No such luck. "I'm sure you know." Joel trailed after Ryo as they got out of the elevator and hurried into the garage. "It's a type of wizard who makes a pact with a kitsune. I'm hoping to do that with you because I need your help."

"Aren't you mixing up Asian legends and that deal-with-demons game we started designing last month?" Ryo reached his car and paused beside it, key in hand. "Look, if you leave me alone, I'll drop this subject, too. And consider seeking professional help. Or at least get away from the computer more."

"Nice try, but I'm not giving up."

"There's a flaw in your plan, isn't there? To make this alleged pact, you said you'd have to be a wizard, which would require magic to exist."

"Magic does exist." Joel's cheerfully assertive tone turned solemn. "I have reason to know it does. I'll prove it to you soon enough."

To Ryo's relief, his coworker backed off when Ryo unlocked his car door and slid into the driver's seat. As he struggled through Baltimore traffic for the first few minutes after exiting the garage, he panicked at the thought that Joel might follow him home. Turning onto the freeway on-ramp, Ryo released a pent-up breath and laughed at himself. Since his potential pursuer knew where he lived, a car chase would serve no useful purpose.

Which meant he might get an unwanted visit at any time. What did that last pronouncement about magic mean, anyway? Maybe Joel actually was coming unhinged. Ryo revolved the unpleasant possibilities in his mind as he drove around the Baltimore beltway to Interstate 97 and south to Annapolis. He reached home with no sign of Joel's car on his tail. Ryo hurried inside and locked the door behind him, releasing the tension in his chest with a long sigh. He stripped off his clothes as soon as he made it to the bedroom. Sure, he could transform while wearing them, but this way was more relaxing. A minute later, he sat in the middle of the floor as a fox instead of a man.

As usual, smells and sounds instantly sharpened, while colors faded to pastels. The comforting scent of his lair enveloped him.

Can't go out like this now. Have to wait for dark. He'd let himself get lulled into carelessness lately, taking risks like transforming outdoors in daylight. Drained by the stress of the clash with Joel, he curled up on the throw rug next to the bed, covered his muzzle with his tail plume, and fell asleep.

When he woke, the sky visible through the window showed the rose and violet of sunset, and he found himself in human form. He stretched arms and legs stiff from lying on the floor with only a braid rug for padding. *Damn, I really should quit doing this.* Ravenous from expending energy on the change, not to mention that it was past dinnertime anyway, he dressed in gym shorts and a T-shirt, then went to the kitchen to throw a steak under the broiler. With no viable plan for handling Joel, Ryo's mind reverted to Shannon and the upcoming weekend. Between getting harassed by a wannabe magician and spending most of two and a half days in a convention dealers' room, the prospect of helping Shannon staff the sale table sounded better every minute. Maybe Joel, given breathing space, would reconsider what any rational person would dismiss as a harebrained idea. Meanwhile, if nothing else, a couple of days away from home would allow Ryo time to figure out his next step. At least at the hotel he'd be a comfortable distance from his unwanted "friend" and surrounded by other people all day.

Not to mention spending time with Shannon. That proximity could prove either a plus or a minus. Plating the steak with the potato he'd microwaved while the meat broiled, he caught himself smiling at the thought of her bouncing ponytail and all the other bouncy bits. Curved in all the right places, she stood only a few inches shorter than he, so if he ever kissed her, he wouldn't have to bend over too far.

Don't go there! He had good reason to avoid getting close to women, especially one who turned him inside out the way she did. For one thing, sexual excitement, even more than other kinds of emotional stress, was likely to trigger the loss of a grip on his human shape. Not only that, if legends he'd read and the hints his mother had dropped were true, erotic intimacy with a human female could pose a worse problem. Folktales claimed kitsune were irresistibly alluring. If a woman responded to his desire, how could he be sure her feelings were genuine instead of magically induced? In the past, when he hadn't yet learned caution, he'd had some close calls along that line.

Even in the not so distant past, such as the evening when he'd let his office mates talk him into going to a bar with them. Three women, out of the blue, had practically invited themselves home with him, two of them female coworkers and one he'd never met before. Sure, maybe some guys would consider those incidents missed opportunities, but he got no pleasure from the idea of seduction by what amounted to a supernatural roofie power.

So we'll keep the relationship friendly and professional the way we have all along. No problem.

After dinner, he sent Shannon an e-mail reassuring her he'd be at the con hotel Friday morning, as agreed, and stay on task all weekend. As soon as twilight fell, he went into his miniature back yard, opened the gate just far enough for a fox to slink through, and—having first checked that nobody was close enough to peek over the fence this time—changed shape for a pleasantly mindless run through the woods bordering nearby Back Creek.

Chapter Three

A background buzz of conversation hummed in Shannon's ears as she set up her display in the ContrariCon dealers' room around noon on Friday. The large, brightly lit space contained several rows of tables in the middle as well as more lining the walls, many of them not yet occupied. It wasn't quite twelve, and the room wouldn't open for business until mid-afternoon, so the only other people present were fellow vendors who'd also arrived for an early start setting up. As she exchanged smiles and greetings with dealers she knew from previous conventions, she plugged in and switched on her laptop while silently fretting over Ryo's continued absence.

Stop thinking like that, she admonished herself. *There's plenty of time yet. He could've gotten stuck in traffic. He promised he'd be here, and he will.*

Not all guys were like Owen, her college boyfriend. In fact, probably most weren't. She had no reason to expect Ryo to let her down the way that loser had. Elena's voice echoed in Shannon's mind with the often-repeated admonition, "Just because you fell for one man who'd lie about the sun shining on a rainy day doesn't mean you should write off the entire opposite sex." Anyway, worrying about Ryo on that basis would be irrational, because he wasn't a boyfriend, just a friend and partner. *Unfortunately. No, wrong thinking!*

Suppose they did develop a closer personal relationship that later cooled off? They would still have to work together on the graphic novels, and how awkward could that get? All the fun would fade from those late-night video chats she looked forward to so much.

Shannon opened the web page displaying the covers of the latest two volumes of *Raptor and Vixen*. The jewelry vendor at the table on her right glanced over and said, "Fantastic artwork."

With a smile and a murmur of thanks, Shannon pulled a stack of print-on-demand paperbacks from the box she'd lugged in earlier. Just as she started setting them out, Ryo strode into the room. She greeted him with a wave she hoped looked casual. *Of course, he showed up. Why wouldn't he?* In high school, infected by her mother's worries about her father's frequent no-shows and late homecomings, Shannon had suffered a perennial fear of getting stood up for dates, a mishap that actually happened once, sort of. The boy arrived an hour late for a Sunday picnic because his family forgot to switch their clocks to Daylight Saving Time. *That was thirteen years ago. Get over it.*

As Ryo walked toward her, she let herself admire his lean form, shown off by tight, black jeans. He wore a black T-shirt with a portrait of Raptor and Vixen, identical to her own. *No harm in looking, is there?* He took his place behind the table and helped arrange the books, propping one copy of each volume on a small stand with others stacked behind it. Working alongside, she sneaked a glance at him, enjoying the way their comparative heights made it necessary to look up but not too far, so he didn't loom over her.

"Did anybody stop by to talk to you yet?" he asked.

"Just a few people I've run into at other cons." Noticing how he scanned the area and repeatedly paused to stare at each of the two doors, she said, "Why? Are you expecting anybody in particular?"

Ryo shook his head, avoiding her gaze. With a mental shrug, she returned her attention to the task at hand. After fifteen minutes of watching him twitch whenever somebody walked into the room, though, she couldn't resist questioning him again. "What's wrong? If you've got a problem you want to talk about, I'm listening. What are friends for?"

"Nothing, really." He rearranged a couple of books before glancing at her, then looking toward the main entrance again. "Nothing that'll affect our work."

Shannon decided not to push. He had a right to keep his private worries to himself, didn't he? She reminded herself she had no reason to doubt his claim that, whatever the trouble was, it wasn't related to their partnership. After they finished setting up, she suggested getting lunch together, although she half expected him to decline.

"Sure," he said. "We've got almost two hours until we open for business."

She returned his smile, careful not to show her mild surprise at his acceptance. This lunch amounted to only the second time he'd agreed to hang out with her for a purely social rather than professional purpose. Although he acted as if he enjoyed her company, he avoided face-to-face interaction more often than not. *The mixed messages are enough to make me dizzy with the head-spinning,* she thought as they walked down the hall to the hotel's casual bar-and-grill.

****

Ryo sneaked appreciative glances at Shannon's legs under her denim miniskirt. The way the black T-shirt clung to her breasts also offered a view worth lingering on. He reluctantly dragged his attention away from the alluring sight. Sharing lunch shouldn't be a problem for him, but letting himself dwell on her physical appeal might undermine his control. *We can do friend stuff together. I have to be satisfied with that.* Still, he couldn't avoid inhaling her rose-scented cologne, mingled with her individual feminine fragrance.

In man shape, his sense of smell didn't equal the keenness of his fox nose, but it did exceed an ordinary person's. Well before they entered the bar-and-grill, aromas of beer, fried meat, and human bodies wafted toward him. They overwhelmed Shannon's scent, probably a good thing. The hostess led the two of them to a booth in the rear and left them to scan the brief menus.

As soon as they'd ordered—cheeseburger and fries for him, a light pasta dish for her—Shannon unfolded her copy of the convention schedule. "We'll both want to attend some panels, so we should divide up table-staffing duties ahead of time."

He got out his own copy, and they ran down the chart discussing which sessions each of them couldn't bear to miss. "Same as always," he said. "The programming committee is telepathic." At her quizzical look, he continued, "They know exactly which events I want to see most and make a point of scheduling them opposite each other."

She laughed. "True that!" They agreed they'd attend Friday night's costume contest and Saturday evening's concert together, when the vendors' area would be closed anyway, then roughed out a plan for staffing their table the rest of the weekend. "Remember, our appointment with Harvey Wright, the editor, is tomorrow at eleven. He said he'd meet us in the dealers' room."

Ryo didn't miss the note of anxiety in her voice. He hoped she was worrying only about the meeting itself, not whether he'd show up on time. "Right, I'll be there, bells on. So what do you think—is the contract a sure thing?"

She tapped on the table. "Don't jinx it. But you read the e-mails from Six Continents at the same time I did. They've made a tentative offer. All we have to do is not screw it up."

He imitated her "knock on wood" gesture. "It'll be awesome to have our stuff in bookstores. And the advance will be nice, too, however much it turns out to be. Not that I plan to quit my day job anytime soon."

A troubled expression passed over Shannon's face before she said with a wry smile, "Good plan. Speaking of that, how long have you been doing game design?"

"I started fooling around with graphic design in high school. I took a double major in art and computer science at the University of Maryland, and I got lucky with the job search. Got hired by the company right out of college." Devouring the last of his fries, he noticed she hadn't touched the garlic bread that came with her pasta. "If you don't plan to eat that…"

With a sidelong glance at his empty plate, she pushed the bread over to him. "Feel free. Must be nice to be able to eat anything you want. Typical male high-powered metabolism, I guess."

Actually, it was the shapeshifting that burned

calories in such high volume. He squelched the impulse to protest that she didn't have a thing to worry about in the weight department. He might not know much about women in general, but he knew any comment on that topic could lead him into a minefield.

"As far as jobs went, I sort of had the same kind of luck," she said. "I majored in English literature, planned to go to grad school and teach college English, until I woke up to the state of the PhD job market. Something like ten applicants for every opening. Meanwhile, I'd been working summers plus part time during the school year in a bookstore in Severna Park, so when the owner, Elena—a family friend—offered me a full-time salary and benefits, I jumped at the chance. It sounded like a better life choice than mailing out a hundred copies of my CV while quoting Shakespeare in between asking, 'Want fries with that?' I'm the bookstore assistant manager now." She sighed, staring down into her iced tea glass. "That job's evaporating, though."

"Ouch. What happened?"

"Money trouble. Elena can't afford to keep the store going." She added with a faint smile, "So I hope our books turn into bestsellers and get made into a hit animated series."

"Here's to that." He raised his glass, and she clinked hers against it. "But I'm not sure I'd quit the day job even if they did. I'm lucky to have work I enjoy that I can do from home most of the time. If the series took off with Six Continents, though, I could afford to visit my mom in Japan more often, which would be cool."

"Your parents aren't together?"

"Not since I started college. I think the marriage had been going downhill for a long time, and they were just waiting for me to get launched before they officially ended it." Encouraged by Shannon's sympathetic murmur, he continued, "My dad's a retired naval officer. They met when he was stationed in Japan early in his career. They loved each other, for all I could tell—what does a kid know about that stuff?—but the relationship deteriorated over the years because Mom was never completely happy away from her home." He couldn't mention the other, more important reason: His father never seemed to fully accept his mother's nonhuman nature. "They didn't fight, at least not where I could hear them. There was no yelling, just a lot of coldness. Even as a self-centered teenager, I could sense the distance."

"It must be rough, not being able to see her."

"I've flown over there twice, but it's hella expensive." Having long since adjusted to the situation, he didn't mind talking about it. "We keep in touch with video chats and social media. It works out okay."

"I can relate, sort of. My father was a naval officer, too, and my parents almost broke up when I was in my late teens. He had a gambling addiction, but while he was on active duty, he had it under control. After he retired and took a high-paying civilian job, it got worse, maybe because he had money to throw around. Lies, secrets, coming home at all hours, driving the family into debt—" She blinked away tears and took a sip of tea. "Things eventually improved, though. He went into therapy, they got counseling, and they stayed together. They're fine now, living in a senior condo complex in northern Virginia." A flush spread over her cheeks.

She'd never shared so much personal information with him before. Warmed by her gesture of trust, but figuring she was embarrassed at blurting it out, he tried for a lighter tone so she wouldn't regret opening up. "So we've got something else in common. We're both Navy brats. What are the odds?"

"Considering this area and Norfolk are East Coast ground zero for Navy retirement, not all that bad," she said. "My older brother went into the military, too—Air Force in his case. Joined the enemy, so to speak." She grinned. "He's married and stationed in Colorado now."

Ryo returned the smile, glad to see her relaxed again. *Friends can discuss personal topics without getting uptight, can't they?* "My dad retired to West Coast Navy retirement ground zero, San Diego. We keep in touch online, and I fly out to visit him every year or two." Getting together that infrequently made it easy to avoid forcing his dad to cope with Ryo's kitsune half. Sure, he knew both of his parents loved him, yet even as a small child he couldn't miss how his father sometimes winced at the sight of a little boy involuntarily transforming into a fox cub. Ryo had been as relieved as his folks when he got old enough to develop some control.

Not that he could reliably hold an intended form even then. One afternoon during his first week in public school, he'd found himself changing on the way to class after lunch. He ducked out and hid in an adjacent vacant lot just in time to keep from getting caught in fox shape. When he didn't show up in the classroom, the staff searched for him and finally called his parents. His mother arrived, tracked him down, coaxed him into reverting to human form, and took him home, claiming he was sick. After giving him a couple of hours to recover from the trauma, she'd coached him through multiple cycles of changing back and forth. Later, she'd trained him in breathing exercises to calm himself and hang onto control, a technique that helped a little but never worked as well as the two of them hoped.

He wrenched his thoughts away from the traumatic memories and picked up the dessert menu. "Want anything else?"

Shannon shook her head. "We better get back to the dealers' room." She waved at the waitress, who dropped off the bill a minute later. Separate checks, as Shannon had insisted despite Ryo's offer to pay.

The instant they stood up and started toward the exit, he glimpsed Joel in the doorway. For a second Ryo hoped he was mistaken, misled by his own fears. But, no, that was his coworker, all right. *What's he doing in this hotel? Looking for me? How did he know I'd be here?* Ryo's pulse raced. Of course—during the past few weeks, he'd mentioned the upcoming convention several times at work. He'd even made casual comments about his plan to sell graphic novels in the dealers' room. *That'll teach me not to bring up personal stuff in the office.*

He sprang to his feet and muttered an incoherent excuse to Shannon about needing to go up to his room for something. "I'll join you at our table later."

She scowled at him as he barely restrained himself from sprinting toward the exit. Drawing attention by openly rushing wouldn't do him any good. Luckily, Joel was occupied with talking to the hostess. Ryo skirted the edge of the room and ducked into an empty booth while Joel followed the woman to a table near the bar. Just as Ryo slipped out of the booth and edged toward the door, Joel turned in his direction.

It was too much to hope the other man hadn't glimpsed him. With a startled look followed by a wide grin, Joel popped up from his chair. Ryo picked up his pace, darted between two people waiting to be seated, and emerged into the corridor. There he broke into a trot. With the frequency of eccentric behavior at cons, nobody seemed bothered by a man running in the hall as long as he didn't bump into people. When he reached the elevators, he found a nearly packed one about to close. An obliging man in an ebony panther costume held it open for Ryo, who dashed inside just as Joel rounded the corner in pursuit.

Ryo let out a long breath as the door shut and the elevator started rising. Heat flooded his face, and his ears sizzled with what felt like static electricity. He recognized the sensation as magic. *Damn, my fox ears are growing.* He resisted the temptation to check the transformation by touch, a gesture certain to attract the gazes of his fellow passengers. The panther noticed anyway. "Wow, great cosplay. Those look totally real."

Ryo managed a weak smile and a murmur of thanks. At least, if he had to suffer such a lapse, this was the place for it. The one woman in the elevator scanned him with open admiration. He might have felt flattered if he hadn't known the appeal almost surely sprang from his kitsune pheromones, not his looks or personality.

By focusing on the techniques his mother had tried to teach him—not easy, when he had trouble concentrating from the stress of his plight in itself—he managed to avoid changing any further and forced his breath into a normal rhythm by the time he reached his floor. He hurried to his room, half expecting Joel to pop up and intercept him. *Don't panic, idiot. He couldn't possibly know what floor you're on.*

Convincing himself he was safe for the moment, Ryo stretched out on the bed and willed his ears to revert to human shape. *Sure, I'm safe now, but I can't lurk in here the whole weekend. If I don't get back to Shannon soon, she'll skin me alive and use my hide for a fox-fur stole.*

****

Waiting for the dealers' room to open, Shannon sat at the table with fists clenched in her lap and gritted teeth. *What the heck is wrong with him?* Upset stomach, maybe? She couldn't think of any other legitimate reason he'd rush out like that. She'd give him the benefit of the doubt and trust that he'd either show up or call her soon. He had her number, and her phone was on, so he had no excuse for not communicating.

Under the background hum of conversation, she greeted the jewelry seller on her right and complimented the racks of Renaissance-style costumes the man on her left was setting up. When the venue opened for browsers, she forced an inviting smile and made eye contact with passers-by, trying to strike a balance between welcome and blatant salesmanship.

About half an hour after opening, she was chatting with a girl in an anime T-shirt about the art displayed on the laptop when Ryo walked in. Shannon tossed him a pretend-casual wave and continued the conversation with the potential customer. When the girl meandered down the row with a *Raptor and Vixen* flyer in hand, Shannon stared up at Ryo, keeping her face blank and choking down the words she wanted to snap at him.

"Sorry about running off, back there in the bar. I saw somebody I'm trying to avoid. Nothing you need to worry about."

"Why? You owe him money?" she asked lightly. *Or is it a she? Old girlfriend?* She mentally shook off the random thought. Sure, Owen, her college boyfriend, had been too much of a coward to admit he'd violated their pledge of exclusiveness by dating someone else behind her back. That disaster had nothing to do with Ryo. *Paranoid much? That happened nine years ago. Totally irrelevant now.*

He answered her half-joking question with a wry smile. "Not that simple, unfortunately. But I won't let it affect our project."

"Better not. You know how much the Six Continents deal means to me." She brushed aside her lingering embarrassment over what she'd spilled earlier about her job crisis and her family's dysfunction. What had possessed her to open up that way anyhow? On the other hand, he'd shared bits of his past, too—an encouraging development.

"It means just as much to me. I won't let you down." With a brief squeeze of her forearm, he took his seat next to her behind the table.

He removed his hand quickly, his face reddening. A blush warmed her own cheeks. Evading his glance, she unnecessarily straightened the nearest stack of books.

The crowd of people wandering through the dealers' room brought a welcome distraction. For the next hour, both Shannon and Ryo were kept busy describing their characters and showing off their work to prospective buyers. They even sold three copies of the trade paperbacks, not a foregone conclusion with all the surrounding competition for con-goers' bucks. She noticed, though, that he frequently cast nervous glances around the room, often pausing to focus on the two doors. Maybe he really was worried about avoiding someone. *Well, why should I doubt his word on that? But who could be causing him that much trouble?*

She finally asked outright.

Ryo sighed. "He's a guy I work with, Joel Brady, who started bugging me about confidential stuff I can't go into. He followed me to the con. That's why I ducked out all of a sudden after lunch."

She remembered seeing a man with sandy hair and wire-rimmed glasses enter the bar, then jump up and leave right after Ryo did. "He must be super obsessed with whatever it is, then. Sounds like a real pain."

"To say the least." Ryo's gaze darted over the crowd yet again. "But maybe he's given up for now. If he shows up again, though..."

"You'll vanish again. I get it, but I hope you won't make a habit of it. One of us has to watch the table continuously until dinnertime or risk losing sales. Such as they are." She tapped the far from overflowing metal cash box.

They spelled each other a couple of times to take breaks in turn. After returning from a session on shapeshifters in folklore, Shannon admitted to herself she felt relieved to find him still on duty. She'd half expected him to abandon his post.

At the end of the afternoon, he said, "Sorry again about my flakiness. Let me make it up by treating you to dinner."

For a couple of seconds she hesitated, unsure about accepting a "treat." Didn't that come perilously closely to a date with him? On the other hand, wasn't that what she wanted—to wade into deeper waters than professional friendship? *Heck if I know. What can it hurt to stick a toe in the pool?* She accepted.

"Cool, and we can go to the masquerade afterward."

She nodded agreement with that suggestion. How much trouble could she get into, emotionally speaking, watching a costume contest in a packed auditorium? Yet she couldn't resist an occasional lingering look at him while they packed up their wares and spread a cloth over the table to indicate they were closed for the evening. The bright overhead illumination brought out deep red highlights in his wavy, black hair. He had amber eyes, almost golden, a color she'd never seen in human eyes before. But yummy looks weren't everything. Was she cutting him slack for his erratic behavior because of his physical appeal? Or, on the other hand, was she being too hard on him because of her own hang-ups?

Quit overthinking. She picked up the cash box and her laptop and bade him a casual goodbye before heading upstairs to freshen up for dinner.

Chapter Four

They met half an hour later at the more upscale of the hotel's two restaurants. Ryo had changed into black slacks with an open-necked polo shirt bearing the logo of his game company on the upper left. Shannon noticed his gaze sweep over her, from the V-necked blouse to the denim miniskirt and her exposed legs. *Does he like what he sees?* If so, why didn't he make a move? How could she sort out her own feelings if he didn't make his clearer? She shook off the thought and followed the hostess to a corner booth with an electric candle glowing on the table.

She ordered a shrimp salad, listening enviously as Ryo went straight for the steak and lobster. How did he stay so thin while eating so heartily? "What about wine?" she asked.

He briefly mulled over the wine list. "Well, okay, I guess. White? We both have seafood coming."

Why did he sound reluctant? If he didn't drink at all, he would simply say so, wouldn't he? "Sure. Chardonnay?"

To her mild surprise, he ordered two glasses instead of a bottle, the more economical choice. With the wine, the waitress set a basket of bread between them. Nibbling on a slice, Shannon asked Ryo more about how he'd gotten interested in game design.

"Since I was a typical videogame-obsessed teenage

boy and liked to draw, it felt like a natural path. I was always that kid who sat in the back of the room sketching cartoons during class instead of taking notes." He finished his first piece of bread and slathered butter on a second.

"I can imagine. Did Vixen start then?"

"An early incarnation of her, after I got giant robots out of my system."

She laughed. "There's a thought. Maybe in the next story arc Raptor and Vixen should battle an invasion of giant robots."

He chuckled. "That could make a great animated feature."

"Do you think we'll ever get a film version?" she asked. "Or a computer game? Maybe you could talk your company into designing one."

"Or we could create an indie game, but that would take big bucks to produce. If we do decide we want to expand into visual media, we should look for an agent."

"First things first. At this point, the mass market books feel like a dream."

"True dream," he said as the waitress delivered their dinners.

"I'm still trying to convince myself it's real," Shannon said. "I'll believe it when I see our signatures under the publisher's on that contract. For now, where do Raptor and Vixen go from here? We can't let their character development stall, and the fans keep trying to ship them." Although the series had a strictly niche audience, it did boast a core group of avid readers who expressed their opinions with rabid enthusiasm. A significant percentage of those wanted to see Raptor and Vixen in a romantic relationship.

"Granted, we need to move in a new direction. They can alternate rescuing each other from supervillains only so often."

"I'm open to having them fall in love," she said as she drizzled dressing on her shrimp salad.

He cut into his steak, which oozed red. "They're two different species, though."

"Our fans accept the idea of animal-shifting heroes from an alternate universe, and that's a problem?" She'd already dropped ambiguous hints in previous issues that an attraction might exist between the two characters, to lay groundwork for just such a potential development. "We've established they love each other as friends, so why not take the next step?"

"You believe cross-species mating could work?" He asked the question in a surprisingly serious tone.

"Why not? Even if they can't interbreed, they could share romantic love. Anyway, if they did have sex, we wouldn't have to worry about the details. It would happen offstage, since we're not writing erotica." Blushing, she shifted her gaze from his face to her plate, but not before noticing a flush redden his cheeks, too.

They talked about future story ideas through the meal. When she finished her wine, Shannon ordered a second glass. After an instant of hesitation, Ryo did the same. "Here's to living dangerously." When the refills arrived, she caught herself watching his mouth as he sipped from the glass. Their eyes met, and heat flooded her skin. He immediately looked away. She deflected the awkwardness with a random remark about the hypothetical game their series might spawn. Ryo's answers became more absent-minded, while he scanned the dining room as nervously as he had during lunch.

"Are you that worried about the guy, whosis, you were trying to escape from earlier?"

Ryo replied with a jerky nod, "Joel Brady. I keep expecting him to materialize from thin air."

"Exactly why is he stalking you, anyway? I mean, aside from the confidential parts you can't discuss."

"We have a fundamental disagreement about a project he's pushing and I'm not in favor of. He won't let it go."

"Wow, to follow you to the con, he must be really obsessive."

Another furtive glance toward the exit. "About this, he definitely is."

At Ryo's request, the waitress handed them dessert menus. Shannon sighed. "This flourless chocolate cake looks yummy, but…"

"Oh, come on, you can live dangerously, too, for a change." He gazed into his empty wineglass, then directly at her. "I'll get one, too. Let's order them to go and eat dessert in my room. No worries about Joel interrupting us there."

Does he mean more than he's saying? Probably not, she decided. At a convention, a hotel room served as a meeting area as much as sleeping space. Glad for anything that might stop Ryo from acting like a road runner on the lookout for a coyote, she agreed to his suggestion.

After they'd left the restaurant with their boxed cake slices and made it to the elevator, he let out an audible breath of relief when the doors hissed shut. She didn't comment, figuring if he wanted her to know further details about why that Brady guy worried him so much, Ryo would share them without prompting. They rode up to the fourth floor and walked to his room in silence.

The room mirrored her own, with a king-size bed, flat-screen TV, mini-fridge, desk, easy chair, coffee table, and small couch. The open drapes displayed the evening sky fading toward twilight, streaked with rose and violet. She settled on the couch beside him, grateful for the imaginary border between the bed and the sitting area. Between bites of cake, they talked more about the chances of their work expanding into other media.

"We can daydream to our hearts' content," she said after a while, "but you know we won't get much if any input into games or films. Not unless we make them ourselves."

"Games, I can do. Movies, not so much. If I could sell the idea to my company, I might get to design the game." He paused to lick a fleck of chocolate off the corner of his mouth.

A shiver coursed through her. How would his tongue feel on her lips? *Danger ahead!* As she'd considered more than once, if their relationship heated up but cooled later, the working partnership could fall apart. "Listen to you," she said with a nervous giggle, "counting our eaglets before they hatch."

"What kind of babies would Raptor and Vixen produce if they did mate? Winged fox cubs hatched from eagle eggs?" He polished off the last of his cake.

"I'm almost tempted to write that scenario just to see you draw it." To avoid the sight of Ryo licking chocolate from his fork, she concentrated on finishing her dessert, too.

"Considering the fans of a certain major film franchise don't seem to have a problem with dragon-donkey hybrids, it's not so farfetched."

He set his empty box on the coffee table, then took hers from her and did the same with it. Turning toward her, he clasped her hand before she could withdraw it.

His skin felt fever-hot, a heat that radiated up her arm. *On the other hand, like he said, sometimes we should live dangerously.* She swayed closer to him.

"Magic," he murmured. "Magic can do almost anything."

He cupped her cheek with his free hand. He leaned in, giving her plenty of time to draw back if she chose.

She didn't. Instead, she parted her lips, waiting. His lips brushed hers. The heat spread over her whole body and flared at her core. His tongue teased hers, and she twined one arm around his neck. Her nipples peaked and tingled. Twisting sideways to close the space between them, she couldn't suppress a sigh of pleasure when he drew her into a loose embrace that tightened as she snuggled up to him.

Her eyes drifting shut, she ran her fingers through the dense pelt of his hair while he deepened the kiss. Waves of sensation rippled through her. As she moved her hand downward to skim over his cheek, fuzz tickled her palm. Whiskers? Surely she would have noticed if he'd been unshaven. Besides, this growth felt more like velvet than sandpaper. She opened her eyes.

Ryo flinched and pulled back. In the twilit dimness relieved only by the light from the overhead fixture just inside the door, his skin definitely looked lightly furred. Not only that, his teeth looked, well—*sharp*. She scooted to the end of the couch.

Ryo snapped his mouth shut and covered it with one hand. Springing to his feet, he mumbled, "Sorry—not feeling well all of a sudden. I'll see you tomorrow morning. Sorry!" He scurried to the bathroom and slammed the door.

Staring after him, Shannon stood up, suddenly lightheaded, and gripped the back of the couch to steady herself. *What's gotten into him? And his ears—why do they look the wrong shape?*

Did he expect her to leave just like that? Assuming he was actually sick, he would have asked for help if he'd wanted it. So, yes, he apparently did expect her to clear out. Well, she wasn't about to beg him to let her stay. Tears prickling her eyes, she grabbed her purse and stomped out.

In her own room a few minutes later, she flopped face up on the bed and waited for her pulse to slow and her head to stop buzzing with hurt and confusion. When she'd calmed down, she forced herself to consider the situation rationally. Either he'd told the truth about a sudden attack of sickness or he hadn't. If so, he would probably call her when he felt better. If not, what had possessed him to act that way? He'd been as into the kiss as she had, no doubt of that. If he had some issue that prevented him from taking their relationship to the next level, why wouldn't he come clean about it? For that matter, why would he initiate a kiss in the first place?

Silly question. Same reason I responded, even when I know mixing collaboration with romance could be a recipe for disaster. That problem aside, if her previous record was any indication, she had a talent for picking the wrong guy.

She was evading the bigger question. What had she seen in those last few seconds? *He had fur and fangs.*

His ears were turning pointy. What is he? A vampire or werewolf or something?

With a humorless laugh, she sat up, wrapping her arms around her knees. *Been reading a little too much fantasy?*

She had to have imagined or hallucinated what she'd thought she saw, but why? Two glasses of wine wouldn't have that effect. The idea that Ryo might have drugged her drink was too absurd to contemplate. For what motive? Furthermore, if he had, he wouldn't have run away from the result of his nefarious deed. Okay, she'd simply spaced out for a second and over-interpreted an optical illusion. Chalk it up to neurotic ambivalence about getting involved with him.

She'd suffered a freakish reaction unlikely to repeat itself. The more immediate concern was that their plan to attend the masquerade together was a washout. *The heck with him. I'll go by myself.*

In the main auditorium a few minutes later, she snagged a seat near the front for a good view of the contest. Overheated from the clash with Ryo followed by the rush to get to the auditorium before the program started, she welcomed the chilly draft from the air conditioning on her bare arms and flushed cheeks. Chatter from the audience blurred into a dull roar like waves on a beach. Ten minutes after the scheduled starting time, a burst of music quieted the crowd, and the MC walked up front to welcome them. While he rattled off a succession of SF-themed jokes, costumed competitors lined up on the right side of the large room. Shannon watched with only half her attention as mythical beasts, anime characters, fairy-tale creatures, and heroes and villains from various film franchises strolled, marched, shambled, or danced across the stage.

Maybe next year Ryo and I should enter as Raptor and Vixen. That is, if we're still working together then. She couldn't get her mind off that final disastrous minute in his room.

In the intermission while the judges retired to decide the winners, and a musical group performed parodic songs about currently popular fantasy and science fiction TV shows, her gaze wandered around the auditorium. She caught sight of a man who looked familiar, walking slowly down the center aisle.

Isn't that Ryo's nemesis? Yes, she couldn't mistake the husky, sandy-haired man in wire-rimmed glasses, especially since he wore a shirt with the game company's logo, like Ryo's. Among all the other people milling around, he didn't draw any particular attention as he paused to scan each row of chairs. He roamed the room in a meandering search pattern for a while, then walked out a side exit.

He did seem to be looking for Ryo. *Persistent, isn't he? But is that enough to send Ryo running for cover at the sight of him?* Surely the trouble between them must consist of more than a disagreement over a work project. *Unless Ryo's just being neurotic about the whole thing. Not that it's any of my business.* He had labeled the problem "confidential," so he must have solid reasons not to discuss it with her.

His nagging presence in her thoughts left her too preoccupied and depressed to care about the outcome of the contest. Instead of waiting to hear the winners announced, she retreated to her room. Just as she reached it and bolted the door, her cell phone rang in her purse.

****

Barricaded in the bathroom, Ryo listened to Shannon storming out of the room. His ears, now completely pointed and furred, twitched at the noise of the door closing behind her. Doubled over, he shuffled out of the bathroom, as the change swept over him. With a groan, he released his grip on his human form and melted into animal shape. He ran in circles between the armchair and couch, lashing his plumed tail, until he exhausted his pent-up frustration. He flopped down on the rug, panting, and forced his body to transform from fox to man. Although he still had vulpine ears and teeth, he stripped off his clothes as soon as he had the appendages to do so. In the process, his tail vanished, and his ears shrank and re-formed.

He stretched on the bed, naked, and clenched his jaws, willing the fangs to revert to blunt, human teeth. The fragrance of Shannon's rose cologne still lingered in his nose, along with the sweet musk of her natural scent. With a sense of smell more acute than an ordinary man's even in human form, he'd been unable to avoid noticing her arousal. She wanted him, maybe as much as he craved her, but how could he know whether that desire sprang from within her or from his innate kitsune allure? Of course, she'd opened up about her personal life more than ever before. Didn't that mean something beyond mere physical attraction? *Damn, I should never have drunk that second glass of wine. I should know better by now.* The blend of alcohol and sexual excitement inevitably dissolved his self-control.

How much had she seen in that last minute or two? With luck, she would convince herself she'd imagined whatever anomalies she'd glimpsed, as most people usually did when confronted with the impossible. He would learn her reaction soon enough anyway, since he couldn't hide from her the rest of the weekend. He owed it to her to lend his support in the meeting with the editor.

Rolling over, he buried his face in his arms. *I'll be lucky if she ever speaks to me again.* After wallowing in misery for a while, he sat up and scowled at his phone, hooked to the belt of his discarded slacks. Dealing with her wouldn't get any easier if he put it off. The longer he delayed, the worse impression he'd make. He pulled on his undershorts, grabbed the phone, and scrolled to her number.

She answered on the third ring, squashing his cowardly hope to leave a message instead of plunging into a conversation. "Well?"

He flinched at the ice in her voice. "I just want to apologize. I had a sudden attack of upset stomach. Maybe it was the lobster."

"Sorry to hear that." Her clipped tone sounded far from sympathetic. "Will you be okay for the meeting tomorrow?"

"For sure. Wouldn't miss it. This collaboration means too much to me."

"Fine. See you then." She hung up without waiting for a goodbye.

She was obviously getting fed up with what she probably considered lame excuses for erratic behavior. Come to think of it, maybe he shouldn't have run away after lunch. Going straight to the dealers' room with Shannon would have kept him in a public place, surrounded by people. In that environment, Joel wouldn't openly bring up shapeshifting foxes unless he had become completely unhinged.

If the man showed up again, Ryo would stand his ground and stay cool. *That is, if I don't start sprouting fangs or a tail.*

He couldn't expect Shannon to let another sudden exit pass with a vague apology, yet he couldn't allow himself to be seen half-transformed. *On the bright side, if she stays mad, I won't have to worry about accidentally enchanting her with my supernatural charms.*

Watching his parents' relationship disintegrate should have warned him against making any kind of romantic gesture toward her, much less kissing her. The seductive aura of kitsune lovers was real, as demonstrated by the numerous men who hit on his mother with no encouragement from her. Ryo's father, sadly, had grown more jealous over the years, more prone to see deliberate enticement that didn't exist. Worse, he'd reached the point of accusing his wife of using that enchantment on him, luring him into marriage against his true will.

Almost all the mythology about their kind warned against cross-species liaisons. Sure, there were a few tales of fox women who became loving, devoted wives. In most of the stories, though, the kitsune seduced the human partner, gave him or her an interlude of dreamlike joy, then ruined the hapless lover's life and vanished. The archetypal legend of a man who thought he'd spent years sharing ecstasy with a beautiful bride in a luxurious mansion, but returned to his right mind only to discover he'd been living in a burrow with a fox and a litter of half-human cubs, was only the most extreme of such stories.

Not that Ryo needed to worry about luring Shannon into such a plight. He didn't have the power to create a magical retreat outside normal space and time. No matter how hard his mother had tried to teach him to use the gifts she thought he should have inherited, the results never measured up to her expectations.

Which is probably a good thing on the whole, considering how I keep screwing up the powers I do have.

****

Hanging around the entrance to the dealers' room Saturday morning, waiting for a staff member to unlock it, Shannon let out a pent-up breath in relief when Ryo walked into view. Irritated at herself for expecting him to bail and at him for inciting that expectation, she answered his greeting with a curt nod. Like her, he wore a T-shirt bearing the cover image from the first volume of their series. He'd remembered their agreement to coordinate their outfits for today. In most ways, he'd constantly proved himself dependable, and then he'd pulled those disappearing stunts on the previous day.

When he commented on the sunny weather outside and made a casual remark about the concert scheduled for that evening, she shut him down with a brisk reply. "No time for chitchat. Let's concentrate on setting up the table to make a good impression on the editor."

The disappointment on his face at her rebuff saddened her, but she hardened herself against that feeling. *All business, right?*

At their table, they folded up the cover and got to work. While he rearranged the books at her direction and unlocked the cash box she'd brought with her, she powered up the laptop. After opening several windows with covers and sample pages from multiple issues of the series, she showed him the result. He complimented her on the display, and she returned a brusque word of thanks. With a barely audible sigh, he took a seat behind the table and assumed a mask of bright-eyed welcome.

By now potential customers were starting to wander in. Both Shannon and Ryo made eye contact with each passerby and pitched the series to anybody who paused long enough to listen. As usual, they had to tiptoe along a fine line between friendly enthusiasm and overbearing hard-sell tactics. In the next forty-five minutes, they made three sales and handed out countless flyers to whoever would accept them. Shannon kept checking her watch, counting the minutes until eleven, when Wright was due to appear. Ryo, she noticed, was glancing around the room the way he had the day before, flinching whenever anyone who roughly resembled his alleged stalker came within their field of vision.

Finally she voiced her exasperation. "Are you still worried about that guy from your office?"

He nodded with a sheepish half-smile. "I know he's not likely to make a scene in front of you and all these other people, but I don't want the hassle of dealing with him anyway."

"Can I count on you to stick around until Wright gets here?"

He glanced at his watch. "I'll do my best. I won't make an ironclad promise, but that's the plan." He looked up, his eyes widening in alarm. "Damn, there he is now."

She followed the direction of his gaze. Sure enough, Brady had just entered the room and was heading toward them.

Ryo cursed under his breath again. "Look, I'll be back to meet Wright on time if I can, but I have to get out of here now. Try to stall Joel."

Before she could sputter out an objection, he slipped from behind the table and retreated at a rapid walk in the direction opposite the main entrance. She spun around to glare after him. What was that hanging from his backside? A russet plume of fur that looked like—

A fox tail? Where did he get a tail? Surely if he'd been wearing it when he'd arrived, she would have noticed. She hadn't been *that* distracted. When did he have a chance to put it on?

When she turned back to the table, Joel Brady was standing in front of it. He scanned the books on display. "Cool covers."

She returned a cautious word of thanks.

"I need to talk to Ryo Larsen. Do you happen to know where I can find him at the moment?"

Resisting the urge to glance toward the side exit, she said, "Sorry. No idea." Ryo must have escaped into the corridor already. Anyway, it was perfectly true she didn't know where he'd gone.

Brady apologized for bothering her and walked away, headed for the main door.

He doesn't look very scary. Why does the sight of him turn Ryo into a nervous wreck?

Chapter Five

Weaving among the stream of people in the hall, Ryo fled toward the elevator at a near-trot while he internally fumed at himself for his lapse. So much for his plan to stand his ground at the vendor table. If Joel saw Ryo this way, there'd be no hope of persuading him to disbelieve in the transformation. Ryo could hardly believe his tail had spontaneously popped out in public. At least here the witnesses assumed it was a costume accessory. He cringed to think of the disastrous results if he ever lost control like that at work.

Mom was right. I'll never measure up to full-blooded kitsune standards. Not that she ever said anything like that aloud, but he couldn't miss the implications of her overly patient instructions. She gave up after trying to teach him to construct a pocket dimension. She created a garden outside normal space, complete with a lotus pool arched by a small footbridge, stepping-stone paths winding through green landscape broken up by bamboo growth, and a stone lantern beside a miniature waterfall. She'd expected him simply to expand the boundaries of the garden. His most diligent efforts produced only patches of mist. If he couldn't even master his shapeshifting, of course he couldn't do complicated things like building a secret world. His fox nature was only a handicap, an alleged superpower that got him nothing but trouble.

In her unguarded moments, he'd thought he sensed more sadness than surprise in her reaction to his efforts. After all, he was half human, not a real kitsune. No wonder he'd disappointed her, even if she tried to hide that feeling.

These furious ruminations got him as far as the elevator, just as he glimpsed Joel at the end of the hall. Ryo squeezed in right before the doors closed, forcing a vague smile in acknowledgment of murmured compliments on his realistic-looking tail and ears.

Ears, too? Damn! He got off one floor below his own and dashed up the stairs.

The moment he reached his room and inserted the key card, Joel popped out of the ice machine alcove and rushed to his side. Ryo dodged around him, darted into the room, and slammed the door.

Joel hammered on it.

"What the hell do you want?" Ryo drew several shuddering breaths as he struggled to make his tail recede and his ears revert to normal.

"You don't want me to stand out here yelling through the door, do you?"

Might as well listen to his rant. What can he do to me, anyway? Ryo let in the unwanted visitor, pacing across the room and flinging himself onto the couch without offering Joel a seat. "How did you know where to find me?"

"With this." Without waiting for an invitation, Joel sat in the armchair and plucked a thin, silver chain from under his shirt. A bronze, pentagonal pendant about the size of his palm hung from it.

He held it up, and Ryo leaned forward to peer at the amulet. It was etched with the image of a tentacled creature—whether octopus, squid, or jellyfish, he couldn't tell. "What's that? And make it snappy, please. I've got places to be." If he didn't show up for the meeting at eleven as Shannon expected, she'd never forgive him.

"It's a long story, so I may not be able to manage *snappy*." Joel lounged back in the chair. "First off, I told you I knew magic was real, and this is why."

"Cut the crap. I don't have time for this." Ryo stood up.

Joel brandished the pendant. "Freeze. Except for breathing and so on."

Ryo did. He couldn't move, except to open his mouth to yelp in protest.

Before he could get out another sound, Joel said, "You can unfreeze. But if you give me any grief, remember I can stop you anytime."

Sinking onto the couch, Ryo said, "Okay, talk." *I'm the last person who should be surprised at authentic magic. But how did he get hold of what's obviously a powerful talisman?*

"You probably know I've gotten into the habit of browsing thrift stores, antique shops, and so on for unusual objects to base game items on."

Ryo nodded, recalling several mentions of such items in brainstorming sessions.

Joel went on, "I ran across this amulet in a tray of miscellaneous costume jewelry a couple of weeks ago. It was rattling around loose without a chain, so I bought this one separately later." He fingered the silver necklace, then went on, "I discovered the pentagon's qualities by accident."

"How?"

"The day I bought it on my lunch break, I came back to the office and caught Brenda, who has the cubicle on the other side of mine, sneaking a candy bar out of my desk. When I told her to stop, she not only stopped, she froze. I experimented with a couple of other commands—don't worry, nothing painful or humiliating—and she obeyed them."

"Whoa, freaky," Ryo said, fascinated despite his anger over being trapped.

"You bet. Finally, I ordered her never to snitch from my stash again and to leave without remembering anything that happened."

"Did that work?"

"Sort of," Joel said. "Later I noticed her giving me funny looks, like she was confused, so I think it might've worn off. Anyway, she must have been shaken up knowing she'd been caught, if she did remember, because no more candy went missing."

"I bet you experimented on other people after that." Ryo doubted anybody could resist such a temptation.

"Sure. Not at work, though. I discovered I have to focus on the person I'm commanding, and if I stop concentrating, the orders don't stick for long. I haven't totally figured it out yet. How long the effect lasts seems to vary widely. Still, it would be super convenient if I wanted to take up a life of crime."

"Which you don't, I gather." Ryo allowed a tinge of sarcasm to creep into his voice. "You have a perfectly ethical motive. You just want to turn me into your familiar because you read somewhere about kitsune-commanding sorcerers. Even if that stuff were true, do you seriously think I'd effectively agree to become your pet? What do you want from me, anyhow?" As Joel had mentioned earlier, a kitsune-mochi formed a pact with a fox shapeshifter to wield power for him. Even if Ryo had possessed the gifts of a full-blooded member of his mother's species, he didn't have the slightest interest in binding himself to someone that way.

"That's a little complicated." Joel leaned back on the couch. He took off his glasses, polished them on the hem of his shirt, and put them back on. "Almost a year ago, my uncle died. He never married and didn't have any nephews or nieces other than me, so he left me his house on the South River in Edgewater."

Ryo estimated that would be located only twenty minutes or so from his own home.

"It's a huge, rambling place built around 1900, and when I moved in, it was stuffed to the rafters with, well, *stuff*. Uncle Tim wasn't exactly a hoarder, but he was an accumulator. He collected all kinds of things— gemstones, fossils, art works, you name it—but never classified or organized them in any systematic way." With a wry smile, Joel said, "I probably inherited that gene. After I started scouring secondhand shops for game inspiration, I kept up the habit just for the fun of it. Anyway, I've been sorting through the house all these months."

"Which has what to do with magically binding me?" With a sidelong look at the door, Ryo speculated on the chance of making a break for it, but Joel pointedly kept one hand near the dangling amulet.

"I'm getting to that. I've whittled down the piles little by little, getting significant items appraised, donating some things, keeping some, selling others. The main interest Uncle Tim constantly returned to was books, thousands of them. I'm talking floor-to-ceiling shelves in almost every room, closets overflowing. I've sorted a lot of the valuable volumes, and when I'm sure I've exhausted that category, I'll sell most of the rest in bulk to a secondhand book dealer. There's one particular collectible I'm looking for, though, and I can't find it."

Is he ever going to get to the point? "Are you sure it exists?"

Joel nodded. "Uncle Tim showed it to me once and said he especially wanted me to have it. A first edition of H. P. Lovecraft's collection *The Outsider and Others.* It was easily the most valuable book he owned."

"And you want to sell it for big bucks."

Joel shook his head emphatically. "I don't need money that badly. I plan to keep it as a memento of him. What I want is to make sure I don't accidentally let it go with the bulk sale."

While Ryo sympathized with that motive, it didn't make up for Joel's highhanded behavior. "I still don't see where I come in."

"Remember that time a few weeks ago when we went to a bar after work to celebrate Mark's birthday?"

"Oh, that." Ryo had let himself get talked into downing one drink more than he usually risked. He thought he'd escaped the consequences. *Obviously I was a tad too optimistic there.*

"I don't think anybody else noticed your ears getting pointed and furry right before you rushed out, but I did. So, just out of curiosity, I researched kitsune myths. When this amulet fell into my hands, I couldn't help but think it was serendipity."

"Sure, the first thing anybody in that situation would naturally think of would be using magic to enslave a coworker like your personal genie."

Joel grimaced. "Please—nothing like that. I just need help."

"To do what?" Ryo sneaked another glance at his watch—past eleven. *Yep, I'm doomed.* In confirmation of those qualms, his cell phone rang.

"Turn that off," Joel snapped.

Ryo's fingers automatically carried out the order.

Smoothly reverting to the main conversation, Joel continued, "From what I've read, kitsune have a wide range of powers beside changing between fox and human. I mentioned some the other day, and you denied having any." He counted them on his fingers. "Invisibility, foxfire, superhuman strength, irresistible sexual magnetism, retrieving desired objects, making people get lost, possessing them, even speaking through them like a medium. Not to mention creating an illusion or reality—it's not clear which—of a place outside normal space. Like one legend I read about a beautiful, mysterious woman who lured a man to her luxurious mansion for a night of passion. When he woke up the next morning, he found himself on a pile of rotting leaves in a graveyard. So did the house exist, or was it a hallucination she generated?"

"You believe all that?" From his mother's words and actions, Ryo knew the truth of the legends. It surprised him a bit that his coworker swallowed the mythology whole, though.

Joel shrugged. "Some of the stories may be exaggerated, but I figure a lot of it's true. The beliefs have to come from somewhere, don't they? What interests me is the part about finding desired objects."

"I get it now. You expect me to track down your missing book like a bloodhound or something."

"Right. If you have that ability, it should be a breeze for you."

Ryo sighed. "And as I told you when you brought it up the first time, I don't. I'm only half kitsune. Like I said, if I could become invisible or hide in a pocket dimension, you wouldn't have caught me this easily. I can change shape and create foxfire, not that I have perfect control over either one. That's all. You'll have to figure out another way to unearth your first-edition Lovecraft." He started to get to his feet.

Joel brandished the amulet. "Stay."

"What, now you think I'm a dog instead of a fox?" Ryo involuntarily resumed his seat.

"Maybe you've never tried hard enough. If I gave you a direct order to use that power, maybe it would work."

"Interesting concept. I have no idea. Keep in mind, you're not exactly putting me in a mood to cooperate."

"You'll want to," Joel said, "if you remember you're stuck under my control until I decide to let you go." He made the threat in an almost apologetic tone rather than the gloating voice of a comic-book villain.

"Are you sure? Didn't you say you have to focus on your target for the magic to keep working? Maybe you can march me down to your car and drive to your house, but it sounds like the minute you take your attention off me, I'll be free to move." Despite his frustrating predicament, Ryo smiled as the funny side of it occurred to him. "Haven't quite thought through your cunning plot, have you?"

Joel frowned, mulling over that point. "Okay, so I'll have to keep giving you fresh commands. I'll manage somehow. Look, why not agree to help me and save us both the trouble? Once I've got the book, I'll leave you alone."

Yeah, right. He'll get a taste of magical power and then just give it up. "Let me go, leave me alone from now on, and I'll forget this ever happened. You're wasting your time anyway."

"You keep insisting you don't have the powers. What if you're wrong?" He held up the pentagon and intoned, "I hereby order you to believe that if you need to, you can do anything a full-blooded kitsune can."

For a second, Ryo wondered whether that harebrained stunt might actually work. He suspected his own doubts about his abilities, combined with his mother's disappointment, had hampered the flourishing of his gifts. His constant fear of exposure if he let his kitsune nature run wild probably didn't help, either. Joel's command didn't make him feel any different, though. "Nice try, but no dice. What's your next move, mighty sorcerer?"

Joel glared at him. "Shut up and let me think."

****

Harvey Wright strode up to Shannon's table promptly at eleven and introduced himself, insisting she call him "Harv." Apparently in his forties, he was a man of average height and build, with sable-brown hair and beard, brown eyes, and tortoiseshell-rimmed glasses. His black polo shirt bore the Six Continents Media logo, a stylized Mercator projection map of the world. She shook hands with him, hoping her palm wasn't clammy with nervousness. "Ryo suddenly felt sick and had to leave. He should be able to meet with you soon, though." *I hope. It could even be true.*

The editor suggested they adjourn to the bar to

discuss the proposed deal. He admired the laptop display and the book covers while she left a message on Ryo's cell phone and also wrote him a note stating where she'd gone. As she locked the cash box and covered the table with the cloth drape, the editor said, "I've noticed you have an attractive, well-established web platform and a solid reader base. Those are definite pluses."

She thanked him for the compliment, and they strolled to the bar, where they managed to grab one of the last open tables. Clearly, lots of people tried to beat the lunch crowd, thereby defeating the purpose. She got a soft drink, while Harv ordered a beer. "I'm in favor of buying your series for e-book and print," he said, "and the rest of the staff is on board, too. We just need to work out the details." He mentioned a surprisingly generous advance payment.

She managed to express her gratitude without babbling effusively.

"Don't worry. We're not planning a rights grab. We like to deal with animation studios ourselves, but you two can keep control over audiobooks, translations, and merchandise like T-shirts, action figures, et cetera. If I were you, I'd get an agent for that kind of thing."

"We've been thinking about it."

If I can pin Ryo down long enough to think straight about anything. She squelched her simmering exasperation over his flaky behavior and forced herself to focus on the conversation.

After a free-ranging discussion of the proposed contract, Harv checked his watch and said, "I have to get ready for a noon panel. This evening Six Continents is hosting a party along with a couple of other companies. Can you and Ryo attend? I'd like to get his input firsthand."

Shannon didn't miss the hint that non-attendance by Ryo would make a negative impression. "We'd love to. Let me try him once more before you go." She called Ryo's cell, which went straight to voice mail again. She left a terse message about the party invitation.

Harv jotted the location and time details on a business card he handed to her, and they strolled out of the bar. "I'm surprised your partner isn't answering his phone, even if he doesn't feel well."

"Maybe he had to lie down for a while and turned it off." *That's all it better be.* "I'll go up and check on him."

"Good idea. I need to meet him in person before making a final decision. He does fantastic work, but the company would have reservations about signing an artist who's not completely reliable."

Acid welled up in her throat. "He'll come to the party. I'll make sure of that."

"Great, see you there." After a farewell handshake, he strode down the hall toward the program rooms while Shannon hurried to the elevator. If Ryo was genuinely sick, she would apologize for disturbing him. If not, she wouldn't leave without a complete explanation.

****

For a minute Joel stared at Ryo, who simply stared back, magically compelled to silence. Finally, Joel said, "Cancel that command. Answer truthfully: You really can't do most of those things mentioned in the legends?"

"I've never been able to so far. My mother had many of those gifts, but she's a full-blooded kitsune and a two-tailed one, at that. Like I said, casting foxfire is about the extent of my ability. Burning your house down wouldn't be much help, would it?"

"Shut up again already." After a moment's thought, Joel said, "Well, it can't hurt to try anyhow. Let's go."

Unable to speak, Ryo arched his eyebrows. Joel said, "We'll go to the garage, pick up my car, and drive to my house. You'll do your level best to conjure up that object-finding power. Once we've found the book, I'll release you."

Ryo gave him a skeptical look. Joel sighed. "Okay, you can talk, but don't even think about yelling for help."

"Have you figured out how to keep me from escaping the minute your concentration lapses?" Ryo followed his captor into the hall. He wasn't tempted to test whether that last clause constituted an order, since he knew if he tried to disobey, he'd only get silenced again.

"That's my problem."

"So it is," Ryo said in an assumed carefree tone. In fact, he wasn't too worried yet, certain the other man would eventually get distracted enough to let him break free.

Joel glared at him. "Go to the elevator."

Walking on, Ryo said as they turned the corner at the end of the hall, "Won't you look sort of conspicuous waving that thing around and giving me orders if we run into other people on the way down?"

Hesitating several paces from the elevator, Joel cast a dubious glance in the direction of the stairs.

"Maybe you should have taken elementary villain lessons before starting this project."

Scowling, Joel opened his mouth, probably to bark another order for silence. At that moment, one of the elevators down the hall opened, and Shannon stepped out.

"Ryo? What on earth is going on?"

At the sound of her voice, his heartbeat accelerated, and heat surged through him. His ears and buttocks sizzled with electricity as the former elongated and the latter sprouted a tail. Joel, brandishing the amulet, glanced wildly from Ryo to Shannon and back again.

Freed from the magical compulsion, Ryo dashed for the stairway entrance. Both Shannon and Joel yelled after him. Fortunately, with her calling his name, he couldn't distinguish the words Joel was shouting, which doubtless consisted of an order to halt. Ryo wrenched the heavy door open and ran down the steps. Seconds later, the other two clattered behind him.

****

Shannon gaped at Ryo's ears and tail. *He didn't have those a minute ago. Where did they come from?*

Deciding to shelve that question for now, she rushed downstairs alongside Joel Brady. "What are you doing? Why are you chasing him?" Maybe Ryo's reluctance to deal with this weirdo wasn't so irrational after all. When they reached the first stairwell, she jumped in front of the man. "Hold it right here and explain yourself." Not that she knew how she'd stop him if he chose to shove past her.

He grabbed her arm. When she batted him with her free hand and tried to jerk loose from his grip, he raised the pendant he was wearing and said, "Freeze."

To her amazement, she couldn't move. Her arms even stopped flailing around, petrified in the position they'd held when he had spoken. She swayed, off balance with one foot on tiptoe.

71

"You can stand straight," he said, letting go of her, "and breathe and blink, but not talk or scream."

Her leg muscles obeyed. She gulped a breath and swallowed.

Halfway down the next flight of stairs, Ryo pivoted, ran back up, and knocked Joel sideways. Joel released the pendant to catch himself, landing on hands and knees. Shannon instantly regained the ability to move. She retreated to wedge herself in a corner, her head spinning. As Joel scrambled to his feet, Ryo sprinted down the stairs.

As he ran, a pale glow shimmered around him. His outline wavered and melted, then coalesced into the shape of a small animal with dark copper fur, a white-tipped, bushy tail, and black paws, muzzle, and ear tips. *A fox? He turned into a fox!*

Joel gripped the pendant and opened his mouth. Without pausing to consider, Shannon thumped him in the side with her purse, then shoved him against the wall. Although dizzy with confusion, she figured the thing Joel wore had to radiate some kind of magic, crazy as that sounded. She couldn't let him shout a command before Ryo got out of range, however far that might be.

When she looked for the fox, he'd fled out of sight. *Good, he's probably safe for the moment.* It apparently didn't take much to break Joel's control over his victims, so it seemed likely he needed to be near people to command them. She ran in the direction fox-Ryo had gone, hoping to get a head start before Joel gathered his wits. Two landings and flights down, she caught up with the animal.

"Ryo? Is that really you?" *Am I dreaming? Hallucinating?*

The fox yipped and wagged his tail. With an inviting look over his shoulder, he scurried down the next stretch of stairs. Hearing Joel's footsteps on the landing above, she hurried after Ryo. *What the heck, if I've fallen down the rabbit hole, I might as well go with the flow.* On the chance that this was actually happening, she couldn't leave him to fend for himself. He picked up speed, and she raced after him.

Chapter Six

Panting, she caught up with him at the ground floor exit. He pawed at the door. The pursuer's clatter on the staircase grew louder. She pushed the door open far enough to squeeze through it along with the fox, and they emerged into the garage. "Hold on! Explain yourself!"

He replied with an impatient-sounding bark, as if to say there wasn't time, and kept running.

She followed, darting around parked cars and dodging vehicles in motion.

I hope he knows the way out. I also hope nobody notices there's a fox loose in the garage. Pausing behind a pillar, she peeked around it in search of Joel. He'd halted two lanes over to scan the area. At her side, Ryo whined for attention and trotted away. She kept pace with him, crouching as low as possible while looking around for an exit sign. When she sighted one, she alerted the fox with a low whistle and pointed.

Together they raced toward it. Joel must have noticed the movement, for he yelled, "Hey, stop," and broke into a run.

To her relief, neither she nor the fox became paralyzed. The wielder of the amulet must need to be closer, maybe right next to them, for the magic to work. He was catching up, though. She lost sight of him as he circled around the rows of parked cars. When he reappeared, Ryo changed course, and Shannon followed.

Joel cut across their path. Gasping, her legs aching, she angled away from him. Out the corner of her eye, she glimpsed Ryo charging in the opposite direction. Joel hovered indecisively for only a couple of seconds. Instead of chasing the fox, he ran toward Shannon. He was panting, too, she noted with satisfaction, but he still managed to block her at the end of a lane.

Ryo pivoted and dashed toward them. "No! Run away!" she cried. No sense in both of them getting trapped.

He ignored her. Instead, he charged at Joel, who instantly ordered him to stop.

Ryo screeched to a halt. When Shannon advanced on Joel, he said, "You stop, too—what's your name?"

Immobilized, she choked out, "Shannon McBain."

The fox's lips curled back from his fangs in a snarl. With a sidelong look at him, Joel said, "If you don't want her hurt, behave yourself."

Ryo froze.

Joel continued, "You're both coming home with me. Okay, I can't command both of you at once, but I can control Shannon, and I know you won't let anything happen to her. After you do what I asked, I'll release both of you."

Yeah, sure you will. As if he'd let them go free, knowing he possessed a magical artifact. Still, it seemed safest to pretend to comply for the moment. Although he didn't strike her as the violent type, he sounded stubborn and desperate enough that provoking him wouldn't be wise.

He gestured with the amulet. "Shannon, go that way."

Her legs moved in the direction he indicated, parallel to the wall, while her muscles quivered in a vain effort to break the compulsion. "Where are we going?"

"To my car. Like I said, we're driving to my house, where I've got a job for him. If I have to renew control over you at every stop and turn on the way, I will."

"Why? What job?"

"Never mind that for now. The point is, if he wants you safe and free, he'll discover how to use those powers he says he doesn't have."

Baffled, she considered asking him to explain himself—*what powers?*—but, knowing he probably wouldn't answer, she decided to conserve her energy.

Fox-Ryo kept pace with them, his teeth bared in a soundless growl. When they reached a two-door compact car parked in the lane nearest the wall, Joel dug in his pocket for the key. The tension in Shannon's muscles slackened. She turned to flee.

Joel instantly snapped, "Stop. Get on the floor and stay there."

As the magic forced her to her knees, the fox lunged at Joel, bumping into his legs. The man staggered and almost fell, barely catching himself by leaning on the car, but kept hold of the amulet. Shannon sprang to her feet. The fox vanished.

Huh? Did he just disappear into thin air?

An invisible hand grabbed her arm.

****

A furious growl rumbled in Ryo's throat. *Hurt her, will you? Not if I have any say in it.*

A wave of energy surged through him. At the same instant, he shifted from fox to man—and became invisible.

Well, go figure. He commanded me to be able to use my gifts when I needed them. I need them—by my standards, not his—so now I can.

He grasped Shannon's arm, and she shrieked in surprise, while Joel looked wildly around. Ryo launched a baseball-size sphere of foxfire at his legs.

The other man screamed and fell, landing on his side, and let go of the amulet. With Ryo still holding onto her left forearm, Shannon lunged at Joel, jerked on the delicate chain with her right hand, broke it, and snatched the amulet. As Ryo pulled her a couple of paces back, out of the other man's reach, she pointed at Joel and ordered, "Stop there. Sit down, don't move, and be quiet."

Scowling, he obeyed. Ryo willed himself to become visible. He vaguely realized he had a fox's tail and ears, but that was the least of his current problems. Shannon gaped wide-eyed at him. A scent of fear wove through her natural fragrance. "What's going on?" She tugged her arm out of his grip.

"Don't freak out. I'm still me." He glanced at the far end of the lane, where a car was creeping in their direction. *That's all we need, witnesses.*

"Now what?" She stared at Joel, who started to heave himself up from the floor.

"Damn it, give that back." He lurched toward her, one hand clawing the air.

She again yelled at him to stop, which he did with an inarticulate growl of protest.

A fresh wave of anger swept over Ryo. It uncovered another layer of gifts he'd suppressed. Without needing to pause for thought, he clutched Joel's collar and dragged him toward the corner where two walls joined.

Ryo visualized what he wanted, and it appeared—a door, mahogany with a brass doorknob shaped liked a fox's head.

With Shannon next to him, he wrenched the door open and shoved Joel inside. When Joel turned to flee into the garage, Ryo blocked the way and threatened him with a deep-throated snarl. Joel ran down the corridor, around a curve, and out of sight. The door behind them swung shut. Ryo beamed a silent command at it, and it vanished. *Can't have people in the garage noticing it.*

In response to Shannon's look of alarm, he said, "Don't worry, I'll make sure we can leave when we need to." Clasping her hand, he took a step forward.

She held up her free hand in a "halt" gesture. "Hold it. Time out." Her breath came fast and labored. "Is there another exit where he can escape?"

Ryo shook his head. "I don't know exactly what's in here, but there won't be a door unless I make one."

"Then you can take a few minutes to explain what's going on. I'm trying really hard not to panic, but help me out here." She pulled free of his grip and sat on the floor against the nearest wall. "What are you, exactly, where is here, and what's with that weirdo harassing you?" As he took a seat beside her, she pressed the amulet into his hand. "You better take care of this. You're the one who's got experience with magic."

"Not much." With a half-smile, he stashed the pentagon in a side pocket.

"Um—you have clothes on. How do you do that?"

Why is that the first thing everybody asks? "Whatever I'm wearing plus any small objects I'm carrying go into some kind of magic virtual storage space until I change back to human. At least, that's how my mother explained it."

"Your mother is a kitsune?"

He nodded. "It wasn't just the cultural differences that broke up my folks' marriage. Dad never fully adjusted to her nonhuman side."

"That must have been rough on you." She patted his hand. "I know a kitsune is a fox shapeshifter in Japanese folklore, but not much else. This is a little scary, but also kind of cool."

He suppressed a sigh. Would *scary* eventually win out, as it had with his father?

At the moment he no longer smelled fear on her, an encouraging development. "You didn't tell me the truth about yourself," she said. "You let me think, well, all sorts of crazy things."

"And this isn't crazy?"

"I haven't made up my mind about that yet. Half of me expects to wake up any second now."

"I've hidden the truth from everybody all my life, for good reasons. This isn't the kind of thing I could just blurt out. Anyway, would you have believed me?"

"We'll never know, will we?" She reached for his head. "May I?" When he nodded, she ran her fingers over the tip of his right ear. "Wow. It's real," she whispered.

A shiver coursed through him. Catching her hand, he forced words past the tightness in his throat. "We'd better find Joel."

"Why has he been stalking you?"

"Short version: There's a valuable book somewhere in his late uncle's house, and he wants me to unearth it with my alleged kitsune powers."

She arched her eyebrows. "That's all this is about? He's mislaid a book and expects you to find it by magic?"

"I think there's more, even if he believes that himself." Ryo spoke slowly, articulating the idea to himself for the first time, as well as to her. "I think he's fascinated with the idea of magic and excited about seeing it in action. I figure this demand is only a test. So I doubt he'll stop bugging me even if I track down the book."

"He said you told him you didn't have the ability to do that." Her voice held a hint of a challenge.

"I didn't, before. Now I do. When he threatened you, something snapped. Also, I've always worried someone would discover my kitsune nature if I used my alleged powers, and here that ship has sailed." He got to his feet and helped her up. "It's as if a locked cabinet full of the gifts I'm supposed to have suddenly got opened."

"Like throwing fireballs and turning invisible?"

"Among other things," he said, "though I could already make fire. Maybe now I could even unearth Joel's lost book, not that I want to do anything to reinforce this obsession he's developed. Speaking of him, let's get moving. There's only so far he could have gone."

As they followed the corridor around the bend, she scanned the curving walls of dark, polished wood. "You haven't explained what this place is yet. How did you find it? Another feature of your fox magic?"

"I didn't find it. I made it. Mom could create pocket dimensions with whole houses and gardens. Until a few minutes ago, I couldn't do anything like that. She'd be amazed to know I managed this much."

Shannon came to an abrupt stop. "Hang on while I process the mind boggle. Making virtual spaces is standard kitsune stuff?"

He shrugged. "For purebred kitsune, it is."

She shook her head, apparently in amazement rather than denial. "How long will it last?"

"Like I said, I'm new to this. Mom's secret hideaways were permanent until she decided otherwise." Scenting a spike of alarm from Shannon, he added, "Don't worry, this place won't evaporate with us in it. It'll stay put at least as long as I'm here."

"What's in it besides a long hallway?"

He took her hand. "Let's find out."

Around the next curve, they came upon five branching corridors. "What now?" she asked.

"We try one and see what happens, I guess."

He led her down the rightmost hall, which dead-ended in a T intersection. Glancing to the right, he glimpsed Joel turning left at the next branching point. Ryo hurried in that direction, followed by Shannon. That path led to a square room with an opening in each wall, including the one they'd entered through.

"This place is a maze," she said. "You didn't plan it this way?"

"Hardly. You saw what happened. I conjured it up on the spur of the moment. For all I know, it's a reflection of my subconscious or something."

"The walls all look alike. We could wind up where we'd already explored without realizing it."

"Yeah, scurrying around at random won't get us anywhere. I need to track him systematically, which means shifting into fox form."

She raked her fingers through her hair as if to scrub away confusion. "I'm maxed out on freaking at the weirdness for now, so go for it."

A few seconds of concentration shrank Ryo's body and morphed it from biped to quadruped. The colors of Shannon's clothes faded to pastels, while her aroma and the noise of her breathing sharpened. He trotted around the square space, sniffing along the walls. Joel's spoor, sour with fear, assailed his nose. Ryo traced it to the door the man had passed through.

He glanced back at Shannon with an encouraging yip. She followed close on his heels as he trailed his quarry. Three more turns brought them to a spot where Joel's scent saturated the air. Multiple openings led to passageways that each curved out of sight within a few feet. Ryo pawed the floor in frustration and sniffed the air.

Wait—I don't have to track him this way anymore. I know where he's going. The heart of the virtual space would draw the intruder, just as it drew Ryo himself.

He shifted back to human form, noting that the transformation flowed more smoothly than usual, and grabbed Shannon's hand. "We're near the center. He's very close. Shut your eyes."

"Huh?"

"Trust me, it'll minimize the weird." When she obeyed, he closed his eyes, too, and stretched his inner perception to trace the shape of the maze. *Yes, there's the center.* Taking three paces forward, he sensed a ripple in the substance of the wall. With her hand still in his, he stepped through the portal that formed around them.

When he opened his eyes, they stood in an

octagonal chamber lined floor-to-ceiling with mirrors. He led Shannon across the gleaming hardwood floor, about ten feet wide, to the opposite wall. Their multiple reflections flickered around them. "You can look now."

She opened her eyes and stumbled at the visual barrage. "What's this?"

He steadied her with an arm around her shoulders. "We're in the middle of the pocket dimension. Joel will show up anytime now." Ryo stared at the oval gap where they'd entered. As he'd expected, seconds later Joel, gasping in barely controlled panic, staggered through it. Ryo silently commanded the portal to vanish. Next he summoned invisibility to conceal him, wrapping an arm around Shannon to shelter her. She flinched for an instant when he faded out of sight but then relaxed into his embrace.

Joel spun around and pounded on the mirrored wall. When no escape route appeared, he lurched along the perimeter, knocking on the unbreakable mirrors and shouting curses. He didn't seem to notice Ryo and Shannon, who sidled out of his path as he completed the circuit. *My invisibility must be shielding her from him somehow.*

"What's wrong with him?" she whispered.

"This place belongs to me, and he wasn't invited. Maybe that's why he's going nuts."

"I can't see you, but I can see myself, and he acts like he can't. See me, I mean."

"This use of the magic is new to me, too. Somehow I'm blocking his sight of both of us. Which is a good thing even if I'm not sure why."

Still whispering, she said, "What now? Staying stuck in here with him doesn't seem like a viable strategy."

"I can get us out anytime. I have to do something about him, though."

Joel, sweaty, his chest heaving, stumbled across the middle of the chamber. He continued to ignore them. When Shannon spoke in a normal tone, he didn't react. "Now that your kitsune powers are working, isn't there some way you can calm him down and make sure he won't hassle you with crazy demands again? If you can conjure a maze out of thin air, it seems like you could do that."

After mentally riffling through the list of abilities Joel ticked off earlier, Ryo said, "Maybe so." His mother had confirmed the reality of the fox possession lore but, after his failure to manipulate magical space, she'd decided the other advanced magics weren't worth trying. Now he seemed to have leveled up in power, though. He canceled the invisibility. What he planned would take all his concentration. "I think I can do this if you support me. Don't let go. I'll need you as an anchor so I won't lose myself." He clasped Shannon's hand in a firm grip.

She squeezed his fingers and edged closer to him. "What are you going to do?"

"If it works, I'll explain afterward." He fixed his gaze on Joel. "Look at me. Sit down and listen."

Exuding a miasma of fear, Joel stared at him. "What? Where did you come from? How the hell did I get here?"

Ryo imagined extending invisible tendrils to envelop the other man and exert pressure on his mind. "Sit down and be quiet. Everything will be all right."

Joel retreated to the nearest wall and slumped to the

floor. He shifted his fear-widened eyes away from Ryo.

"Look at me," Ryo repeated. "I won't hurt you. Open your mind." He visualized twining those tendrils around Joel's head and lulling the storm of panic. Closing his eyes, he imagined himself painlessly slipping inside the other man's skull.

A chaotic swarm of emotions buzzed there. For a second Ryo recoiled in shock. *It worked! I touched his thoughts. Can't stop now—have to go through with it.*

He decided to alter the visualization. Not tentacles, cables. He linked his mind and Joel's together like a pair of computers. A flood of sensation and emotion rushed along the link. Confusion, fear, avarice, and guilt threatened to swamp Ryo's awareness. The other man's heartbeat hammered inside his head, and for a moment Ryo couldn't distinguish that pulse from his own. Overwhelmed, he flailed against the tide.

I'm drowning!

A warm embrace drew him from the depths. A firm handclasp steadied him—Shannon's. He clung tightly to that support.

I can do this.

He channeled his consciousness down the link again. *Calm, quiet, peace.* The tumult receded.

Listen to me, Joel. Magic doesn't exist. There's no such creature as a kitsune. Forget what you did with the amulet. It was an ordinary medallion with no special qualities. You've misplaced it, but that's not a problem. You didn't need it after all.

The waves crashing through the other man's mind smoothed away. Ryo continued the gentle reshaping process: *Forget you had any reason to believe I'm a kitsune. You don't believe in the supernatural. You didn't witness anything unusual this weekend. When we meet again, you'll see me as a casual work acquaintance, like always.*

Joel's thoughts settled into placid acceptance. *Rest now,* Ryo told him. *When you leave here, you won't remember anything weird, and you won't be upset or worried. Now go to sleep.* The other man's mind went blank.

Link by link, Ryo detached the connections and dissolved the cables. When he finally withdrew into his own head and opened his eyes, Shannon was still clasping his hand. After a couple of deep breaths, she said, "Incredible. For a minute I felt like I merged with you, as if I was inside your mind." Just before the remnants of the link dissipated, he felt her pulse racing with a blend of excitement and fear.

"It was a little scary for me, too, but mainly it was good. You grounded me the way I asked you to." With hands joined, they walked over to Joel and gazed down at him. He slouched in a heap against the wall, apparently asleep as Ryo had ordered.

"What did you do?" she asked.

"Got into his head. I changed his mind—literally."

"Is he okay?"

Ryo nodded. "Just sleeping. He'll be all right, and he won't remember any of the supernatural stuff."

She studied his face with a sidelong look. "You sound awfully sure."

"It worked." He was surprised himself at how confident he felt. "Something clicked, you might say."

She scanned their surroundings. "No door. What now?"

"That's no problem. Stick with me." Holding onto

her, he gazed at the nearest wall. The mirrored surface melted. In three paces, he led Shannon through it.

They stood in the wood-paneled corridor. At a wave from him, the opening behind them flowed shut.

"We have to retrace our path through the halls to get out?" she asked.

He smiled at her with new confidence. "No, we can use a shortcut." He touched the wall, and a door appeared. They stepped from the corridor into the parking garage. With no need to puzzle over what to do next, he waved at the door, and it vanished, leaving only the gray cinderblock wall.

Chapter Seven

Her head spinning, Shannon sagged against Ryo and wrapped her arms around his waist for support. His heartbeat thumped reassuringly in her ear. She drew a quivering breath and sighed it out. "The door's gone." *Was it ever really here? And did he really turn into a fox?*

"Well, yeah. It's not like I could leave it for random people to discover."

She rubbed her eyes and gazed up at him. He didn't have fox ears anymore. "I'm not sure I didn't dream this entire incident."

"Does this feel like a dream?" He enfolded her in a tight embrace and lowered his mouth to hers.

She gasped, involuntarily parting her lips. His tongue teased hers. A rush of heat surged over her. Reeling with the flood of sensation, she clung to him to keep from being swept away. Her pulse pounding in her head and her chest tight from lack of air, she finally had to break off the kiss and gulp for breath.

He stepped back and held her at arms' length. "If that's a dream, let's not wake up."

Slipping out of his grasp, she had to swallow before she could speak. "We have to wake up. Places to go, things to do." She couldn't let herself get carried away by passion until she had answers for the questions of her rational side.

He switched on his phone, glanced at the time display with a dismayed expression, and showed her the numbers. After 5 p.m.

Her pulse stuttered. "Seriously? There's no way we've been inside that magic space—or whatever—all afternoon."

"Most of the legends say time inside a kitsune's lair runs slower than time outside. Apparently that's true. I should've remembered."

His quick shift to cool acceptance of the anomaly annoyed her a bit. "What about Joel? You're just leaving him in there, wherever *there* is?"

"Without my input, the virtual space will eventually disintegrate, and he'll go free."

"How soon?" she asked.

"Since I've never done this before, I'm not sure. It was all mainly theoretical for me until today. Hopefully not until after we leave here tomorrow."

She looked dubious. "Will he be okay for that long?"

"If time runs on a different scale in the maze, it's not as if he'll feel like he's been trapped inside all weekend. Plus, I ordered him not to worry." Uncertainty flickered in his eyes. "At least, I hope it works that way. He's a pain, but I don't want to do him any real harm."

As they crossed the parking garage toward the entrance to the hotel, the reason she'd come after Ryo in the first place surfaced in her mind. "I don't want that either, but I'm glad he's not likely to harass us tonight. We have to meet Harvey Wright at a party."

"Say what?"

"That's what I came up to tell you. On top of that, we have lots to talk about. You not telling me you're a fox shapeshifter, to start with." They hurried through the halls to their dealers' table. "No point in reopening for sales now, so let's go up to my room." She retrieved the cash box from under the cloth and led the way to the elevator.

"Way to take charge. I like it," he said as they rode up to her floor.

She blushed at his teasing grin. "I'm not letting you run off this time."

"I don't want to run." He squeezed her hand.

In her room, they sat together on the small couch between the desk and the window. After catching her breath, she blurted out the first thought that popped into her head. "So that's why you're so good at visualizing beast-people. And why you suggested a fox for Raptor's partner."

He nodded.

"So why didn't you trust me enough to tell me?"

"Was I supposed dump it on you out of the blue? And as I said before, would you have believed it? You'd have thought I was putting you on or out of my mind."

"Well, I almost thought I was out of my own mind when I saw you change. Earlier, I wondered if I was losing it when I saw you with fox ears and a tail at random moments, too." Her stomach churned with a blend of outrage, astonishment, and excitement. *The transformation thing is kind of thrilling, in a way. There's magic in the world!*

"Look, I understand why you didn't want to reveal your secret at first," she went on. "But you could've shared it with me when you started half-changing in front of me. More important, you could have come clean about why you kept vanishing instead of letting me think of you as flaky or worse."

"I didn't want to risk destroying our relationship by freaking you out. I was afraid you'd panic or be repulsed. I can't forget how Dad never completely got used to Mom's…differences. Deep down, he wanted her to act as human as possible, like on that old TV sitcom about the nose-twitching witch." He took her hand. "I didn't want something like that to get between us."

Shannon pulled away. "Now we'll never know how it would have worked out, because you didn't trust our friendship enough to take the risk."

"Give me a break on that, can't you? You're the first person except Joel who's ever found out since I was a kid. Well, plus Thad and Val."

"What? You told my cousin but not me?" That detail felt like a slap in the face, just when she'd begun to accept his rationale for secrecy.

Ryo sighed and covered his eyes for a second before gazing into hers. "It wasn't like that. They accidentally saw me in fox form the same day Joel did, only a couple of weeks ago." He sketched the highlights of an incident when Joel had caught him transforming and Ryo fled to Thad and Val's for refuge. "The magic in the atmosphere of their house attracted me." When Shannon opened her mouth to question that new revelation, he cut her short. "It's complicated. I'll explain that part later. Now, what were you saying earlier about a party?"

She told him about the editor's reaction when Ryo hadn't shown up for the appointment and about the event the two of them were invited to. "He implied his decision depended heavily on meeting you tonight, so don't flake out this time." She smiled to take the sting from the words.

"I won't, now that I don't have to hide my true nature from you. I do worry about the fox traits popping up at awkward moments, though. That's why I avoid groups of people as much as possible. Not to mention going easy on the alcohol."

"You don't have to worry this time. We'll figure out how to handle it together." Now that the most anxiety-stirring parts of the conversation were done, her stomach growled a reminder of the long stretch since lunch. "How about ordering dinner from room service?"

They called for burgers, fries, and soft drinks from the menu. While waiting for the food, she quizzed him further about his double nature. "How long have you known you were a kitsune?"

His eyebrows arched. "As long as I can remember. How long have you known you're human?"

She acknowledged the retort with a self-conscious laugh.

"Mom started teaching me to control the change as soon as I was old enough to understand. When I'd stopped transforming at random, around five, she let me play with other kids under her supervision." He gazed into the distance as if watching a video of his memories. "Sometimes I felt it made Dad uncomfortable to see me frolicking around the house as a fox cub."

Shannon patted his shoulder. "That must have been tough for you." *Maybe I shouldn't have been so hard on him about keeping this stuff secret.*

He shrugged. "It was what it was. Little kids don't know the world should be any different from their experience." A knock on the door interrupted him, so he paused to collect the food and tip the delivery person.

Arranging the items on the coffee table, he continued, "Sometimes my ears or tail, or both, popped out while other kids were around, but of course nobody believed them. Mom taught me at home until middle school, and by then I could suppress the changes pretty well except when I was stressed."

"Judging from the way you've acted this weekend, I guess keeping it under control isn't always easy."

"True that." He took a sip of his drink. "It tends to happen when I get upset for any reason, and of course lapses cause more stress, which leads to more lapses. Vicious circle."

"I'm starting to understand why you avoid people so much." She nibbled on her fries, watching him take two large bites of his burger. "Hey, I bet transforming burns a ton of calories."

He nodded with his mouth full.

"Sounds like a plus to me. Any chance I could learn to do that?"

He laughed. "Sorry. I'm not a movie werewolf. It isn't contagious."

She sighed. "That's what I figured. So before today you couldn't do most of those magical things?"

"Right. Only the fireballs. I think part of my problem was unconsciously living down to my mother's ideas about my half-human limitations. When I saw you in danger, though, something snapped. It didn't matter anymore how many times I'd proved I couldn't make full use of my kitsune gifts. I had to do whatever it took to protect you."

Warmth suffused her at that remark. *Then he does care about me.* Her first impulse was to snuggle up and wrap her arms around him, but she thought better of it.

Talk first, then get physical—maybe. "How do you feel about your powers now?"

He paused in thought for a moment before answering. "Better. Discovering what I could accomplish without those ingrained inhibitions gave me confidence."

"Great, so you should have confidence we can work things out between us."

"I've wanted that for a long time, more than I can say." He clasped her hand. "I didn't dare try to get closer as long as you didn't know about my—my other side."

"Well, if you'd tried," she said, "think where we might be right now."

He flushed, released her hand, and looked down at his plate. They finished off the food in silence.

After they stacked the plates on the tray and took a break to wash up, she rejoined him on the couch and made the request she'd been working up to. "I want a demonstration. Before, in the middle of being attacked, all I saw was a blur and then a fox."

"You're not afraid?" he asked in a hesitant tone.

"Why would I be? You'd never hurt me." True, her pulse was racing, but not with fear. "I need to watch you transform so I can convince myself for sure it absolutely happened."

"All right, if that's what you really want." His hands shook a little as he stood up and peeled off his shirt. "I can change while fully dressed, but it's easier this way." Toeing off his shoes, he emptied the contents of his pockets onto the coffee table. Again a faint glow emanated from him. His shape melted and dissolved into mist. A second later, the fox stood in the man's place.

Shannon exhaled a tremulous breath. "Wow." She

reached out, palm up, to hold her hand under his muzzle. She suppressed a nervous giggle as she realized she was treating him like a dog. "May I touch?"

He gave an affirmative-sounding yip. With a tentative brush of her fingertips, she stroked the side of his neck. The dark russet fur felt dense and soft. *Like his hair in human form,* she realized.

When he leaped onto the couch beside her, she ran her hand down his back and along the plume of his tail. He felt almost feverishly hot to her fingertips. "It's real. I didn't imagine any of it. I wonder how it feels to turn into an animal? I'm almost sorry I'll never know." She stroked him once more, and his body quivered under her touch. *What am I doing? This is still Ryo.* She folded her hands in her lap.

The air shimmered around him again, and he flowed back into the form of a shirtless man. When their eyes met, he glanced away and hastily pulled on his shirt. "Hard to say how it feels," he said, "because it comes naturally to me. Adjusting to four legs and a lower visual vantage point takes almost no time after changing. As a fox, I don't see colors so vividly, but smell and hearing become sharper. A side effect of having a double nature is that those senses are keener in human form, too, though not nearly as much as when I'm transformed." He captured her hand. "Either way, you smell delicious." He leaned over to graze her lips with his.

Swaying toward him, she yielded to the melting warmth that radiated from the point of contact. She rested her free hand on his shoulder to steady herself.

"You taste great, too," he murmured, then deepened the kiss.

She figured she tasted like hamburgers and fries, as he did, which was fine with her. She clung to him as her head seemed to float above her tingling body. When he abruptly pulled away, she winced at the shock.

Touching her only with his hands clasping hers, he said, "Sorry, I don't know what came over me to say that—or do that."

"Why are you apologizing?" She barely managed to avoid screaming. "It was fine with me, or didn't you notice?"

"I don't want to put pressure on you, which I could do without even meaning to." He released her hands and sat back against the cushions.

"What do you mean, pressure?" She shook her head in bewilderment. "I don't get it."

"That's one main reason I haven't tried to get closer to you, even though I wanted to. Well, aside from the problem of revealing my true nature." His lips quirked in a rueful smile. "Believe me, I really wanted to get close."

"So what stopped you?" Exasperation sharpened her voice.

"Kitsune emit an erotic aura that's irresistible to some humans. How could I be sure you weren't responding to me for that reason instead of sincere attraction?"

Wavering between annoyance and amusement, she folded her arms and glowered at him. "Think a lot of yourself, do you?"

"It's not me as an individual. It's a kitsune gift—if you want to call it that—common to all of us and not under our control. I saw it with my mother. Men pursued her even when she did her best to discourage them. That was one of the reasons she and Dad broke up, I think."

Shannon couldn't help sympathizing with Ryo on that point. While an involuntary erotic lure wasn't the same as her father's gambling addiction, she knew how it felt to watch her parents' marriage disintegrate.

"It's happened to me, too. I've been hit on by women I hardly know."

"And from that you jump to the conclusion I can't control my own response to you? I haven't thrown myself at you, have I?" *Not for lack of desire, though. Maybe he has a valid concern.* No, she wouldn't believe a mindless magical aura could warp her free choices.

With a half-smile, he said, "Not so I've noticed. But how could I ever be sure how you really feel?"

"You can be sure because I'm telling you I kissed you of my own free will. Don't you trust my ability to make decisions for myself?" She held his gaze with a challenging stare.

His cheeks reddening, he looked away briefly, then met her eyes again. "I trust you to be honest."

"I hope I can trust you the same way. No more secrets." She scooted closer to him. "Now kiss me." She almost choked on the bold demand, but she had to dismantle his belief that an outside force was compelling their mutual attraction.

He took a deep breath and drew her into a loose embrace. "You're sure?"

She answered with a jerky nod, "What do you want, a written guarantee?" She tilted her head in invitation.

He accepted, first tentatively nibbling her lips, then claiming them in a deep kiss. She twined her arms around him, delighting in the lean firmness of his shoulders and torso. Heat flooded her body, with a tightness in her breasts and a flutter in the pit of her stomach. After a long moment, they broke apart, both gasping for breath.

He had fox ears.

He sprang to his feet and backed away. "You see why I was afraid to get too close to you before? The transformation tends to run wild when I get—uh—excited."

"Not to worry." She struggled to suppress the tremor in her voice. "That's no problem now that I know the truth anyway, is it?"

"You're not repulsed?"

"Of course not. I think it's awesome, even if in a weird sort of way."

"We probably shouldn't rush this, though." He closed his eyes as if concentrating, and his ears melted into their normal shape. "We need to get ready for the party, right?"

She nodded, reluctantly grateful for the respite. "Drop by here at eight, and we can go together."

"Sounds like a plan." He hastily stuffed his things back into his pockets. After a quick hug, as if he still feared lingering over it, he left.

She bolted the door behind him and leaned against it, breathing hard, her pulse racing. She touched her tingling lips.

I'm falling in love with a fox-man.
****

Ryo knocked on the door promptly at eight. Her internal sigh of relief surprised her. *Was I afraid he wouldn't show? I should start trusting him.*

Like her, he'd chosen to wear a T-shirt with one of his illustrations on it. "Great minds," she said, pointing to his chest and then her own.

As she stepped into the hall, he said, "I can't help being nervous about meeting this guy in the middle of a crowd of strangers. Whenever I have to do anything like that, I worry about suppressing the ears and tail, not to mention fangs and random fur."

"Worrying makes control harder, right?" She offered her hand as they walked, and he accepted it. "So don't obsess. Go with the flow."

"Just like that?" He glanced at her with a rueful smile before scanning the corridor as if concerned about being overheard. "Easy to say."

"Have you tried partially changing on purpose and stabilizing it that way? Around here, anybody who doesn't actually see the transformation happening will assume they're fake."

"I never thought about doing that. Holding it stable would be the hard part."

"You've got me to help you now, though." She thought back to what they'd done in the last few minutes before exiting the maze. "Before, I felt as if I were channeling psychic energy to you. If that wasn't an illusion, I could act like an anchor, keep you from losing your grip on the shape you want to maintain."

"It's worth a try." Leaning against the wall, still holding her hand, he closed his eyes. His fingers, at first cool, grew warm, then hot.

I'll bet transforming revs up his metabolism. The outlines of his ears wavered, and they dissolved from human to fox. On the lower part of his body, a plumed tail lashed from side to side.

"Way to go," she said.

He turned his head to check out his tail. "I've never

changed selectively like this on purpose before."

"I knew you could do it." *Well, I hoped so, anyway.* "How about an experiment? Could you transform one but not the other?"

"I never tried." He narrowed his eyes in concentration. A second later, the tail vanished.

"Cool! See, you do have control over the process."

The tail reappeared while the ears reverted to human. Next, tail and fox ears appeared together. "I guess you're right."

"Of course I am. If you feel it slipping, just concentrate on me. I'll be right beside you the whole time."

He squeezed her hand. "Thanks."

They rode the elevator up to the designated party floor. They easily found the suite they wanted by the roar of conversation overflowing through the open door. Inside, a wall-to-wall pack of people shouted to be heard over each other, ramping up the overall volume. Science-fiction-themed music played in the background. Ryo visibly winced at the noise. *His ears must be extra sensitive even when he's mostly human.*

With at least a third of the guests in costume, Ryo's animal appendages drew only an occasional glance. She noticed, with an absurd twinge of jealousy, that women's gazes did tend to linger on him. *Could that supernatural allure really be why he turns me on? No way!* While she had to concede that might have sparked the attraction, now she knew and appreciated him as a whole person.

Shannon caught a glimpse of Harvey Wright on the other side of the room next to a desk that displayed publications from Six Continents Media and the two other publishers co-hosting the event. Noticing her, he waved and started threading a path through the crowd. Shannon and Ryo met him halfway. When they got close enough to hear each other, she introduced him and Ryo.

"Nice ears. Very realistic," Harv said when they shook hands. "Good to finally meet you."

"Sorry I had to bail earlier. I'm fine now."

"Grab a drink, and let's find a quiet corner."

Beverages and nibbles covered a pair of tables against one wall. Ryo passed up the wine and beer for club soda, so Shannon did the same. The three of them retreated into one of the adjoining bedrooms, Harv claiming the desk chair while she and Ryo took seats on the edge of the bed.

The editor reviewed the terms he'd already proposed to Shannon. Next, they discussed the logistics and timing of taking the self-published volumes off the market in preparation for release of the Six Continents reprints. Harv laid out a tentative timeline for several new graphic novels, a schedule she knew Ryo would have no trouble meeting. He'd always displayed the drive of a hardcore workaholic, and now she realized why. With his understandable aversion to socializing, he had an abundance of time and energy for creative pursuits. When the advance figure came up, he was as delighted with the amount as she had been.

Finally, Harv stood up and shook hands with them. "I'll recommend a contract on these terms, and you should hear from us within a week." He rejoined the throng in the main room, while Ryo and Shannon, heading for the exit, picked their way around the edges of the clustered conversation groups.

"You don't want to stay for a while?" she asked him.

He bent to speak directly in her ear, the tickle of his breath sending a delicious shiver through her. "No, thanks, crowds of people still make me jumpy."

With a glance at his vulpine ears, she hooked her arm in his. "You're doing fine. But leaving is okay with me. I can hardly hear myself think."

They cleared a path to the door and stepped into the relative quiet of the corridor. By unspoken consent, Ryo rode to her floor with her. "We're in," she said as they strolled toward her room. "We're going to be rich and famous."

He returned her grin. "I'll be thrilled if we manage one of the above. At the very least, Six Continents is big on pushing for film adaptations, so we might see an animated Raptor and Vixen some year in the not too distant future."

At her door, they both hesitated for a second after she pushed it ajar. She took the initiative to step inside, waving him ahead of her. "You made it through without slipping. I knew you could." Okay, that expression of confidence might be exaggerated, but considering how well things had gone, she figured she could be excused for shading the truth.

"And I think I can undo it at will now." As soon as he finished the sentence, his ears and tail poofed out of existence.

"Do it again."

With a rakish smile, he conjured up the ears and instantly made them vanish.

"See, you don't have a thing to worry about." She hugged him around the waist.

When he wrapped his arms around her to draw her into a tighter embrace, her heart pounded at the pressure of his taut body against hers. With a sense of inevitability, she tilted her head in invitation. He accepted with obvious eagerness. The heat of his lips on hers radiated throughout her body, making her nipples and other, more sensitive areas ache. She closed her eyes to savor the melting sensation deep within her. When she became conscious of his hardness pressing against her, she ended the kiss, struggling to catch her breath.

"Wow." He pulled away to put a few inches of space between them, although his arms remained loosely around her. "You're not afraid of me?"

"Are you kidding?" Disentangling herself, she took his hand and led him to the couch. When they were both seated, she said, "Does this feel like fear?" This time she initiated the kiss.

Endless minutes later, her head reeling, she drew back. He had a tail, fox ears, and a velvet layer of russet fur on his chin. "Oops," he said with a lazy smile. The vulpine features disappeared.

"Way to go." She ran her fingers along his jawbone. "I'm getting to like the ears, though."

His smile faded. "You have no idea how good that makes me feel. But how can we be sure your attitude won't change the way my father's did?"

She leaned back against the cushions with a thoughtful frown. "We can't, can we? How can anybody be sure how they'll feel after ten or twenty or fifty years? All we fallible mortals can do is make promises and try to live up to them." Her parents had fought to heal their damaged union and succeeded. Maybe she should focus more on the healing than the damage.

"I don't know about you, but I definitely fall into the fallible mortal category." As if he'd read her mind, he added, "I'm sorry I thought I had to lie to you, especially now that I know your father failed your mother that way."

She exhaled a long breath, as if dispelling the pent-up mistrust she'd clung to. "We don't have to be like our parents, do we?"

"Right. You can trust that I won't lie to you again, and I can trust that you won't turn against me because of what I am." He raised her hand to his mouth and bestowed a lingering kiss on her curled fingers. "You know I want to stay with you tonight, don't you?"

"I did sort of guess that," she said with a shaky laugh. She couldn't resist a quick glance downward at the visible bulge.

Do I want that? So soon? While her body shouted an enthusiastic affirmative, her brain urged caution.

"The last thing I want is to leave you like this, but I feel we shouldn't rush it."

Torn between disappointment and relief, she nodded agreement. "This is all so new and strange. It's true I'm not scared, but my mind is still boggled."

He got to his feet, still clasping her hand. "We can take all the time we need to process what's happening between us. After all, waiting builds anticipation." He flashed her a smile. "If you need to work through the concept with somebody besides me, you could talk to Thad or Val."

"Because they already know about you?"

"More than that. They had the supernatural in their life before they found out about me."

Shannon stood and walked with him to the door.

"Really? How so?"

"Not my secret to share, like mine wasn't theirs to tell." He brushed his lips lightly over hers. "See you tomorrow in the dealers' room."

She hugged him but forced herself not to linger over the embrace.

"I'd better go before I weaken and change my mind."

Squashing the persistent wish that he would, after he left she bolted and chained the door behind him before she could weaken instead.

Chapter Eight

While staffing their table Sunday morning and packing up at noon, Shannon and Ryo kept their conversation light. Only when they had an illusion of privacy in the garage, loading her car, did she feel free to mention the events of the previous day.

Scanning the bare concrete walls, she asked, "What about Joel? You think he's still in that dimensional pocket?"

"If he weren't," Ryo said, hefting a box of books into the trunk, "I think we'd have seen him. I'll check up on him after I get home. I just hope I can do it without making him suspicious about why I'm suddenly interested in what he's up to."

Shannon paused to brush stray hair out of her eyes. "You're sure he'll forget all about the supernatural phenomena the way you told him to?"

Ryo shrugged. "With luck. I can't be sure, never having done this before."

After they'd finished stowing the boxes and laptop, he dug into his pocket for the pentagonal amulet and offered it to her. "You should have this, in case you have second thoughts and feel you need protection."

"From you? No way."

"Take it anyhow. I'm not totally cool with having used fox possession on Joel, even though I didn't have much choice. I can understand if that creeped you out a little. I'll feel better knowing *you* know I can't have any power over you."

Warmth radiated through her at the tenderness in his eyes. She closed her hand around the amulet. "That's not a worry, but thanks."

He gave her a quick kiss on the cheek, turned away, and strode briskly across the garage. Watching him, she fingered the burning spot he'd kissed.

****

Over the next couple of days, the only contact Shannon had from Ryo consisted of brief e-mails about their current project. Without the amulet, she might have relapsed into dismissing the weirder parts of the weekend as a dream. The conversations with the editor had really happened, anyway. The generous advance made the looming prospect of unemployment and job-hunting less grim. She researched kitsune, astonished to read about the wide array of magical gifts legend attributed to fox shapeshifters. Their power level was linked to the number of tails they had, with nine-tailed kitsune being almost godlike. As far as she'd noticed, Ryo had only one, maybe because of his half-human background.

By Tuesday evening she finally worked up the nerve to phone Val, her cousin Thad's wife. Shannon had misgivings about broaching the topic of animal shapeshifters with someone who wasn't much more than a friendly acquaintance.

After identifying herself on the phone, she said, "Ryo Larsen suggested I should talk to you about him. This is going to sound crazy, I know..." She trailed off, groping for a rational way to phrase her question.

"You found out he's a kitsune," Val said in a

casually cheerful tone.

"Then I'm not crazy? I was starting to wonder."

"You must have a ton of questions. Want to get together and talk about it? We could meet at lunchtime someday soon, if that works for you."

They made an appointment for the next day. Shannon could hardly wait to find out the meaning of Ryo's remark about Val and Thad's experience with the supernatural.

****

Shannon took a long lunch hour on Wednesday and drove to downtown Annapolis to meet Val, who worked in the historic district on State Circle. She found the other woman waiting at the Main Street coffee shop they'd agreed on. Val, around Shannon's own age, with shoulder-length strawberry-blonde hair, bangs, and silver-rimmed glasses, wore a light summer dress and carried a small paper bag. They each bought an iced coffee, and Shannon chose a veggie wrap from the display case.

At Val's suggestion, they sat at an outside table on the brick-paved sidewalk next to the narrow, one-way street. The awning of the coffee shop provided cover from the summer sun, and a light breeze mitigated the humidity. She produced a sandwich and an apple from her bag. "I'm a little surprised you know about Ryo. When we learned his secret, he mentioned he didn't want to tell you."

"He didn't. He bent over backwards to keep me from knowing. That's why I was a little shocked when he told me you and Thad knew." Also indignant at first, but Shannon didn't intend to mention that shameful reaction.

"It happened totally randomly. A man who works in the same company accidentally witnessed him changing into a fox."

"Joel Brady," Shannon said. "He was stalking Ryo at the convention."

"Really? I'd like to hear more about that. Anyway, Ryo ran in a blind panic and ended up at our place. We decided he must have been attracted by the magic in our house."

"Ryo said you already knew about magic, but he wouldn't explain why."

"Yeah, we've known things like that really happen for about a year. We have a spirit cat living in our house."

Shannon almost choked on the bite she was chewing. After swallowing, she said, "A what?"

"She's an immortal white cat who can take human form at will for limited times. I accidentally woke her from a spell she was under."

Val's casual tone boggled Shannon's mind. "Do you often have interesting accidents like that?"

Val laughed. "Believe me, at the time I was completely blown away. At first I thought I was going bonkers, the way you must have felt when you saw Ryo change. It's a long story. Short version, Yuki—the cat—was under a curse, and Thad and I helped break it. Several other yokai—miscellaneous spirits—were involved, including a wolf demon."

"Compared to that, one shapeshifting fox seems almost routine. So your live-in spirit is like Ryo, only a cat?

"Not exactly." Val paused to sip her coffee, as if gathering her thoughts. "Yuki is mainly a cat, and she was never human. She just takes the shape of a woman now and then. Ryo's human, or half human anyway, so he's mortal, and that's his primary form."

"I guess I get it." Shannon's head was spinning by now. She finished her veggie wrap and took a drink of iced coffee while watching the mundane view of crawling Main Street traffic and strolling tourists. "How do you deal with knowing reality is so different from what science teaches, what our whole culture believes?"

"As I said, we've had a year to get used to the idea. Once the crisis with the curse ended, having Yuki around became just a part of our lives. It's not as if the occult pops up at every turn otherwise." Val caught and held Shannon's gaze. "You're worried about adjusting to the supernatural if you get more deeply involved with Ryo?"

Shannon nodded. "I'm falling in love with him." *There, I said it aloud.* About time she admitted she'd been half in love with him since long before their "date" on Memorial Day. "But I don't know how to feel about his nonhuman side."

"Is he a different person now from who he was before you knew this? Did you see any indication he'd ever hurt you? In principle, is this so different from discovering he has a chronic disease or something like that?—except being a kitsune is more of an advantage than a liability. It inspired him to create his Crimson Vixen character, didn't it?"

"Oh, are you a fan of Vixen already?"

"Sure, Thad and I have been following your work for quite a while."

Shannon cast her thoughts over the events of the past weekend. "I know he'd never hurt me. He saved me from Joel." She sketched a quick overview of what had happened at the con. "But that showed me Ryo has powers I don't have and couldn't have imagined. Though I'm sure he wouldn't use them against me, they're still hard to wrap my head around."

"On a mundane level, most men are physically stronger than most women. Yet in good relationships we don't sit around worrying about that discrepancy."

"You've got a point there. I just have to find a way to accept that there's a whole other world underneath the one we know. It's mind-boggling that almost anything could happen, like in Wonderland or fairy tales."

"It's not that extreme," Val said, stuffing her sandwich wrapper and apple core in the paper bag. "After all, since last year Thad and I haven't met any new supernatural creatures except Ryo, which was a positive experience, nothing scary."

"If other ordinary people, like you and Thad, can accept it, I guess I can learn to."

Val stood up and tossed her bag into a nearby trash can. "Why don't you and Ryo come to dinner at our place this Friday? Just casual. You can pass on the invitation to him and let me know."

"Thanks, I'll do that. And thanks for the unique perspective." *It's my job to invite him? Clever way of throwing the ball into my court.*

****

Unable to nerve herself up to phoning Ryo, Shannon transmitted the dinner invitation by e-mail. He instantly replied with an acceptance, and she confirmed the specifics with Val. Late Friday afternoon, he picked Shannon up at her home to drive to Thad and Val's.

"Do you know anything about Joel's status?" Shannon asked as she buckled her seat belt.

"I know he escaped from the pocket dimension," Ryo said, backing out of the driveway, "because he called out sick from work part of this week. I don't know what he remembers, if anything, though."

"What are you going to do?"

"Already did it. Right before leaving home just now, I e-mailed him asking how he's doing. Missed you at the office yesterday, that kind of thing. I used a question about a current project as an excuse."

"Sounds good. If he doesn't mention anything supernatural, you can assume your command to forget it stuck." She shared Ryo's misgivings about letting the issue slide, along with his obvious relief that his coworker hadn't stayed trapped in the maze.

When they got to Thad and Val's home and walked up the front steps, a white cat with a red scarf around her neck was seated on the porch. With a meow that sounded almost like a greeting, she strolled to the door, tail waving. Ryo spoke to her in what Shannon assumed was Japanese.

"That's the spirit cat you mentioned?"

He nodded. She had a momentary flash of doubt—was that detail some kind of put-on after all?—before Thad opened the door to let them in, and the cat vanished. *I was looking right at her. She didn't run inside. She just suddenly wasn't there.*

Mentally shaking off the down-the-rabbit-hole feeling, she concentrated on greeting Thad and Val. A long-haired tabby stalked into the living room, hissed at Ryo, and sprinted out of sight. Val said, "Sorry. You probably smell like a predator to him."

She's so casual about that, Shannon thought. *Will I ever get that blasé about believing six impossible things before breakfast?*

"No problem," Ryo said. "I'm used to it. Dogs react the same way, only worse. That's why I've never had a pet."

"So what can we get you to drink?" Thad asked. "And how do you like your steaks grilled?"

Dinner prep and serving proceeded with general conversation about everything but shapeshifters and magic. Thad and Val asked questions about the convention and the graphic novel series to draw out Ryo, with Shannon tossing in occasional comments. The white cat didn't reappear until they adjourned to the den with dessert, strawberry-topped cheesecake. Curled up in the center of the couch that faced the sliding glass door onto the patio, she stretched and moved to a corner to make space for Shannon, Ryo, and Val.

A high-backed, bamboo papasan chair scooted into the middle of the rug and positioned itself for Thad to sit on. Shannon dropped her fork on her plate and sputtered for several seconds before she could manage articulate words. "Did that chair move by itself?"

Thad nodded, patting the chair arm. "You're not hallucinating. Believe me, I reacted the same way the first time I saw it."

Val said, "It's residual magic from the enchanted scroll that broke the spell on Yuki. It's complicated."

After a bite of cheesecake and a fortifying sip of wine, Shannon said, "And the cat—Yuki—is really an immortal, shapeshifting creature?"

The cat arched her back and meowed in what

sounded like a slightly indignant tone.

"She says of course she is," Ryo translated, "and please don't speak about her as if she isn't here."

Shannon murmured an apology. "You understand her?"

"Yeah, I hear her sounds as Japanese. It must be because I'm half yokai—supernatural creature—myself."

"And I hear them as English," Val said, "because I'm the one who accidentally activated the scroll."

Thad flashed a smile at Shannon. "Welcome to the null-magic club." All four humans laughed.

"I do have possession of a small piece of magic," she said, fishing the amulet out of her purse. "We took it from Joel when he tried to control us with it, and Ryo gave it to me for safekeeping." She passed the bronze pentagon to Val, who showed it to Yuki.

The cat pawed it and vocalized.

Val handed it back to Shannon. "She confirms that it's a powerful talisman. Do you know where it came from?"

Ryo explained how Joel had found the object by chance in a secondhand shop.

Yuki emitted another string of meows. "She says we should be careful with it," Ryo said, "which I already figured out on my own. Even if the effects don't last long, it's still a dangerous temptation, being able to compel people to obey you. That's why I gave it to Shannon."

"Like I'm guaranteed temptation-free, huh?" She asked Thad, "As one null-magic to another, how did you adjust to all this? You obviously aren't freaked by it now."

"After we defeated the wolf demon threatening Yuki, with a lot of help from the spirit of her long-dead boyfriend, we settled down to a new normal." The cat's whiskers twitched at the word *boyfriend*, as if objecting to it. "People can get used to just about anything. Once you accept that things you thought were impossible can happen, you stop worrying about your sanity and move on with your life."

After dessert and further conversation about their respective paranormal experiences, they strolled around the back yard in the twilight, admiring Val's vegetable garden. She sent Shannon and Ryo off with a sack of early tomatoes for each of them. By the time they said goodnight to their hosts, lightning bugs were twinkling in the shrubbery.

In the car, Ryo switched on his phone to check it before starting the engine. "Hey, I've got an e-mail from Joel. He answered my question about the game project, then said this about the con." He read aloud: "I didn't feel great after that convention, so I went to the doctor Monday. He didn't find anything wrong, but I took a couple of days to rest up anyway. My memory of the whole weekend is patchy. Truth is, I don't remember a thing between exploring the dealers' room on Saturday and finding myself in the garage Sunday night. Did I do anything flaky, stupid, or obnoxious? If so, don't hold it against me, okay? Maybe I had a prolonged blackout for some obscure reason, like an attack of forty-eight-hour flu. Meanwhile, on the bright side, I came up with an idea for a new game, a maze with mirrors and shapeshifting monsters."

"So your forget-everything command took effect," Shannon said. "That's a relief."

115

"Without permanently warping his brain, apparently, thank God." Ryo turned on the dome light and typed a reply, which he showed her: "No problem, you acted normal every time I ran into you. You did mention you were worried about a book you inherited from your uncle that was misplaced somewhere in his house. What if I come over sometime soon and help you look for it? Two sets of eyes are better than one."

"Do you think that's a good idea? It won't trigger the buried memory?"

"I don't think so," he said, sending the message. "I don't have to explain how I find the book. If stray memories did surface, I could wipe them again, but I hope that won't happen. Messing with his head once was more than enough."

"And you think you'll be able to use your kitsune finding gift to dig up his lost book?"

"I'm pretty sure I can." Ryo turned off his phone, started the car, and pulled onto the street. "It's got to be easier than constructing a pocket dimension. Anyway, for the first time in my life, I have solid faith in my abilities. You give me confidence." He reached over to touch her hand.

When they arrived at her apartment complex, she invited him in. She managed to suppress a sigh of relief when he readily accepted. He'd never visited her before. Too late, as they walked into the foyer of the one-story end unit, she remembered the newspapers scattered on the coffee table and the unmade bed and basket of unfolded laundry in her bedroom. *Not that he'll necessarily see the bedroom.* A blush warmed her cheeks at the thought.

In the living room, she swept the papers into a pile

and offered him a drink. He'd restricted himself to one glass of wine at dinner.

"I'm not sure I should."

"One more won't interfere with your driving, and you don't have to worry about accidentally changing in front of me, do you?"

He smiled. "Granted. Okay, one drink."

She poured two glasses from the bottle of Riesling she had open in the refrigerator. Seated beside him on the couch, she took the amulet out of her purse and handed it to Ryo. "Now I know I'll never need this. You should keep it." From the way he'd dealt with Joel, she had faith that Ryo would never misuse his inborn mind-control ability, so he could certainly be trusted with the amulet.

"If you insist." He put it in his pocket. "But rather than risk temptation, I'll rent a safe deposit box and lock it up, first chance I get."

"I admit I'd feel better knowing a thing like that isn't rattling around loose for anybody to pick up."

They drank their wine while discussing the terms of the publication contract and their plans for the next story arc in their series. When Ryo finished his drink, he leaned toward her, his fingers lightly curling around the nape of her neck. He stopped with his face inches from hers. "May I?"

"What are you waiting for?"

"Hell if I know." His arms tightened around her, and he claimed her mouth in an ardent kiss.

She opened her lips to welcome the flicker of his tongue. From that point of contact, waves of fire and ice chased each other along her arms and down her spine. When he shifted one hand to her breasts and brushed his fingertips across the taut peaks, electricity zinged through her nerves.

Too soon, they had to stop and breathe. "We can move to the bedroom if you want." Her pulse pounded in her head, and her voice trembled despite her struggle to sound calm.

"Oh, I definitely want. Can't you tell?" He stood, drawing her to her feet. He hugged her to him, letting her feel his hardness through their clothes. "I've craved this practically since the day we met."

Inside, she melted from the heat of his embrace. "I have, too, almost as long. So why didn't you say anything?"

"Like I explained, because I was afraid of influencing you to do things you didn't really want." He massaged her back in expanding circles. "Now I know we've moved past that."

Holding his hand, she led him down the hall to the bedroom. She folded the covers all the way down and sat on the bed. Her gaze fixed on his eyes, she unfastened the top two buttons of her blouse.

He perched on the edge of the mattress a few inches from her. "There's something I need to confess before we go too far. The few times I made love to women in the past, it always ended in disaster. Seconds after the climax, or once right in the middle of it, I started transforming. I had to jump up and run away to keep from getting unmasked. Needless to say, that wrecked any chances of intimacy. So I'm not totally inexperienced, but close."

She suppressed an irrational twinge of jealousy at the idea that he'd been with other women before she'd ever met him. "You lost your grip because you panicked. There's no risk of panic now, is there? Anyway, if you do change involuntarily, we'll work around it."

"You really think we can?"

Her belief didn't rest on thought in the analytical sense, but on the emotion that welled up as she gazed into his eyes. "Trust me on this."

"I do." He scooted closer. "Because you trust me. I never dared to feel this way before."

Between kisses, they unbuttoned and unzipped each other's clothes. An awkward pause followed as both of them peeled off the layers of garments, each getting briefly tangled up in sleeves or leg openings. The draft from the air conditioner cooled Shannon's flushed skin. Her heart racing with a blend of excitement and nervousness, she lay face up, her head propped on a pair of pillows, and scanned Ryo's naked body. He was lean and trim, with a sprinkle of dark hair arrowing down to his groin.

What did I expect, a fur coat? Heat pooled in her core at the sight of his erection.

Lying above her, he skimmed one hand down her side and over her hips while they shared still more ravenous kisses. She couldn't help squirming with impatience as their hands roved eagerly over each other's bodies. His skin felt feverishly hot. Running her fingers through the dense pelt of his hair, she encountered something unexpected and widened her eyes to examine what she'd touched.

He had fox ears. She stroked their velvety tips and felt his responsive shudder down the full length of her body. A plume of fur brushed the backs of her legs—his tail. He flinched and rose onto his elbows. "Sorry."

119

"Relax, it's okay." She twined her arms around him. "You won't change any further."

He nuzzled her neck. "It doesn't bother you?"

She laughed softly at the tickle of his breath as he spoke the muffled question. "No way, I think it's kind of sexy." Actually, the caress of the restlessly lashing tail on her thighs sent a wave of sensuality sweeping over her. "Whatever you were about to do, don't stop now."

His hands and mouth explored everywhere, making her desire spiral higher by the second. He seemed to brand every place he touched. She whispered and moaned, first in encouragement, then entreaty. When he reached her most sensitive spot, ecstatic sensations flooded her whole being. She clung to him as the tide crashed over her.

When she opened her eyes, he leaned on his elbows above her, hesitating. She eagerly arched her hips. "Aren't you ready?"

He ran a hand from the V between her breasts to the triangle of her mound. "More than ready." His hard shaft grazed her thigh. "But what about protection?"

She rummaged through the nightstand drawer for one of the just-in-case condoms she'd stocked up on, with fantasies of a moment like this lurking in the back of her mind. After sheathing him, she opened her arms in invitation. He stretched on top of her again, nibbling on the corners of her mouth. As that playful gesture morphed into a devouring kiss, she let her eyes drift shut as she wrapped her arms and legs around him. He plunged deep inside. As he drove to his peak, another wave swept her away.

At last, panting, he turned on his side, bringing her

with him. She noticed that at some point the vulpine appendages vanished. "Sorry it was so rushed."

She gripped his shoulders and gave him a gentle shake. "Quit apologizing. It was great."

"It should be more relaxed next time." He planted a kiss on her bare shoulder. "Assuming there's a next time." Her heart fluttered at his tentative tone. "Because I realize I've been in love with you since—I don't know, half of forever."

"And I've felt the same way. I just didn't admit it until it ambushed me last weekend." A giggle escaped her, which he cut short with a quick kiss. "So I hope we'll have too many next times to count."

Thank you for purchasing
this publication of The Wild Rose Press, Inc.

For questions or more information
contact us at
info@thewildrosepress.com.

The Wild Rose Press, Inc.
www.thewildrosepress.com